TO Anastasia

S, champion)
Forever!

What magic is afoot?

THE SOCIETY OF TWO HOUSES

William C

THE SOCIETY OF TWO HOUSES

William C. Tracy

Space Wizard Science Fantasy

Raleigh, NC

Space Wizard Science Fantasy
Raleigh, NC
www.spacewizardsciencefantasy.com

Publisher's Note: This is a work of fiction. Names, characters, places, and incidents are a product of the author's imagination. Locales and public names are sometimes used for atmospheric purposes. Any resemblance to actual people, living or dead, or to businesses, companies, events, institutions, or locales is completely coincidental.

Cover art by Luisa Preissler
Interior illustrations by Micah Epstein
Book Layout © 2015 BookDesignTemplates.com

The Society of Two Houses/William C. Tracy.-- 1st ed.
Library of Congress Control Number: 2018905714
ISBN 978-0-9972994-6-5

Author's website: www.williamctracy.com

For Grandad:
Who inspired me to learn everything I can

CONTENTS

PART ONE

The Body

- Maji in the Great Assembly of Species are rare, born at a rate of, hm, one per five million individuals. Most hear only one of the six aspects of the Great Symphony, but one in every sixty maji, or one in three hundred million individuals, can hear two of the Symphony's aspects. It is one's belief these few—the, hm, ones gathered here—have the ability to drive innovation in the Great Assembly, bolstered by a sensitivity to the underlying rhythms of the universe. For this group's final entrance into the Society, please, hm, step forward for the geas to be applied.

Private address by Moortlin, Benish Head of the House of Healing, on the induction of new members into the Society of Two Houses

I stared down at the body of Speaker Thurapo, willing my frozen feet to bring me further into his study. I was supposed to be presenting the prototype model I held, not discovering his corpse.

I clenched my hand involuntarily, then yelped and released my fingers as the scale model of the System Beast dug tiny sharp hands into my palm. The delicate construct, made in the form of a Festuour—like my colleague Gompt—had taken days to build. The pain unlocked my feet and I hurried forward to set the model on a side table—just a little too tall for me, like everything in the Speaker's study.

Though my first instinct was to go to the Imperium guard, I instead closed the study door. I had a few minutes during which the deceased Speaker and I were supposed to meet, before his secretary announced his next appointment. My mind flew through what questions the guard would ask if I alerted them.

Majus Mandamon Feldo, is it? Why were you here to see the Speaker? Why does a majus need approval from the Assembly? Shouldn't this be going through the Council of the Maji?

Even thinking of telling the authorities about the Society of Two Houses made the jingly earworm of the geas threaten to derail my thoughts. The guard would quickly become suspicious when I further choked and fainted instead of telling where my prototype System Beast came from or under whose patronage I worked.

I shook my head, dislodging the music that kept the Society safe. Because of our...unconventional methods, Society maji went through a roundabout process of getting approval from the Great Assembly to introduce our new and disruptive inventions.

Per our usual methods, the head of the Society had 'convinced' the late Speaker not to ask questions about where my colleagues and I got our resources. Even I didn't know how the Society provided so many high-quality metals and logical gearing ratios.

Once available, our System Beasts would be the perfect servants and secretaries. They could haul loads, act as butlers, deliver mail, remind owners of engagements, and much more. However, without a sponsor, Gompt, Kratitha, and I would never be able to supply them to the inhabitants of the Nether. If this murder even hinted at our organization's existence, it would also compromise and taint our research by association. I'd be left with nothing, and the Society could no longer develop innovation without those in power asking severe questions. My heart sped, just thinking about it.

Now, the Speaker who would have sponsored us was dead. I let myself really look at him, sprawled out on the floor. He was an Etanela, half again as tall as me, hence the furniture.

What had happened to him? One hand rose to my mouth, then down to the small beard I was growing out, pulling at the hair in thought. Something in my head was silently screaming, though I had been near violent death before. *Stay calm.*

I had to concentrate—use the few minutes available to figure out what happened. Then I would at least have a way to defend myself against questioning authorities. Otherwise, they would detain me as a suspect, no matter what I said. Any questions would lead to the Society.

There was a pool of blood, slowly seeping into the carpet, and still dripping from the deep cuts which nearly severed the Speaker's neck. His head was at an unnatural angle, wide glassy eyes staring out from his faintly blue face. Though his mouth was open in shock, the blue coloration was natural to the Etanela, not a symptom of asphyxiation. He wouldn't have had time to suffocate before the blood loss to his brain killed him. I tried to push away the nausea threatening to bring my breakfast back. Adding to the mess would only complicate solving Speaker Thurapo's death.

The Speaker and I had corresponded through the Imperium's mail service just the day before, and he'd invited me to show him the model my colleagues and I had created. Introducing innovations developed by the select group of maji I belonged to had to be handled delicately—a dance of avoiding names, places, and methods of experimentation.

Was the Speaker killed to stop me from showing him the little System Beast? Did someone find out about the Society and its methods?

No. That was paranoia bordering on my mentor's level. No one outside of my unique Society even knew what the System Beasts were.

Was this self-inflicted? I couldn't see how. There was no implement here with which the Speaker could have cut his own throat—not like that.

The Speaker's secretary would check on us soon—maybe even open the closed door without knocking. I had perhaps ten minutes—the time in which I would have presented my proposal—before someone else called for the Speaker's attention.

The defining quality of maji belonging to the Society of Two Houses was that each of us could hear two of the six aspects of the Great Symphony, rather than just one, like most maji. Each combination of aspects had its own label. My title in the Society was 'Investigator.' Until now, I thought the titles merely convenient masks for those members not wanting to be identified by name. Now it seemed more ironic.

So—I would investigate, and if I could clear any trace of the Society from Speaker Thurapo's death, then I would go to the authorities. If not, well, I'd deal with that when I got to it.

Wood paneling made the office comfortable, and a dominating Festuour-made rug covered the tile floor. There was one desk, clean save for a writing mat, with a chair on either side. Beside me was the side table where my prototype sat. Both side walls held rows of bookshelves, dusty and obviously little used. The Speaker's body took up most of the floor, splayed across the center of the rug.

I looked at the chronograph—an older invention of the Society—chained to my vest, marking time until I estimated I would be discovered with the corpse. I knelt by Speaker Thurapo's body, careful to avoid putting the knees of my tailored suit in the pool of greenish blood seeping into the rug. I could feel the heat from the blood, and from the body, though the sticky liquid was already coagulating. He had not been dead long, whatever happened. I swallowed bile and leaned in.

Aside from the deep gash in the Etanela's throat—certainly fatal—there was no other sign of a fight. I looked from the body to the closed door of the study, gauging where the Speaker would have been standing.

Falling back on the rug like this meant he was facing the door. Along with his killer? It was pure luck the body hadn't hit the chair pulled out on this side of the Chorin-wood desk. I held one hand out, measuring. Speaker Thurapo's frizzy mane of auburn hair was less than the width of my hand away from one leg of the desk.

I pushed my glasses up my nose, and tried to forget how Thurapo would have been the sponsor for our new company selling System Beasts, and a façade to remove interest in where and how my colleagues and I had developed the idea.

Many of the experiments occurring behind the walls of the mansion where I lived would not sit well in the public eye, yet the Society was a generator of progress. It also had connections—under false identities, of course—to many of the Speakers for the Great Assembly, using its members' reach to exploit potentially embarrassing knowledge. I didn't know what Speaker Thurapo had done, but I hoped his indiscretion had nothing to do with his death. The Society's direct involvement would complicate things greatly.

From information gathered over the short time I had been a member, I knew the Society's efforts had saved people's lives and ended wars quickly and efficiently. Its members had added comforts to our lives like freezing and heating technology and remedies for bacterial infections. If, in the process, a few unknown persons suffered, or a few highly prized resources went missing, what was that against the good of all? Yet I was sure the Great Assembly or the Council of the Maji would not see it the same way.

Time was wasting, and I reigned in my thoughts, looking up to the desk. Someone must have been sitting on this side, speaking with the Etanela before pushing away. The Speaker had come from behind his desk before he was killed. I clenched my jaw. What prompted his death, and why did it have to happen this morning, of all mornings?

A non-majus might have difficulty discovering more in the brief time before they were found. But as an 'Investigator,' I had two advantages: the Symphonies I could hear.

I let the Symphony of Healing fill my mind with faint rising and falling scales. It told me Speaker Thurapo was definitely dead, his complex trills and glissandos degenerating into steady and uninteresting eighth notes.

Conversely, the Symphony of Potential dealt in transferring energy, and as I listened to the fundamental music underlying the universe, I heard residues of people's actions, reactions, and movements. Each one was a traceable resonance, though some were extremely faint.

As I got to my feet and went to the desk, the musical themes of energy became clearer. Speaker Thurapo *had* come around the desk—a glissando and dipping trill in the music—following another body, who was speaking with him. I crossed the rug on the other side of the Speaker's body, stepping over his large boots, pointed out at angles. I looked away from the ghastly wound.

Sifting through the Symphony of Potential, I found another fading theme. Thurapo had been standing just here, and...I listened carefully, trying to separate out one rhythm, like listening to a single string playing in an orchestra. I *thought* his assailant had stood in the doorway, ready to leave, but it was hard to say. Closing the door had partially written over that music. I checked my chronograph again—I had found nothing yet, but there was still time.

Did this other person murder the Speaker? They must have. Could it be connected to showing the System Beast prototype model? The geas protected the Society and—some would say—its unethical practices. It was supposed to be foolproof. I didn't want this extra complication. Just creating the System Beasts had been challenge enough.

Need more information. My eyes, almost of their own accord, were drawn back to the body, my subconscious registering something I'd missed. I wiped sweaty hands on my vest and stepped closer, pulling the hem of my pants away from the ruined section of rug, and Thurapo's throat. The fingers and thumb of the Speaker's right hand were together, as if he had held something. Going by the corpse's open mouth and wide eyes, he had been surprised when he died.

The House of Potential revealed a fading jangle of discordant notes—tight muscles in the Speaker's hand, now loosened in death. The House of Healing repeated an intertwined duet—he'd been holding something made from organic material, like cloth or paper.

I knelt down by his right hand. Another trait of an Investigator was to hear the past energy and biology of an object—like seeing a short way into the past. I listened to the pattern of harmonics between the two Symphonies.

The music of Healing was regular, overlapping chords weaving into a rigidly defined structure. The music of Potential held the fading change in beat that meant the object had been cut or torn from another source. It was probably a piece of paper, taken from a larger source of information—maybe something the Speaker had written? *Finally, another clue.*

I let the Symphony of Potential take the upper hand, retracing the descending melody. It led toward the closed door. So, whoever had killed the Speaker had taken what he held into the hallway and beyond. I checked the timepiece on my vest again. About half my interview time gone.

I opened the door, peering both ways. The short corridor was empty for the moment and I surged outside, closing the door silently behind me. The intersection of Healing and Potential rose out here, the notes more recent. Whoever had taken the paper went this way.

I turned left, following the melody. This hallway was in the lower level of the Dome of the Assembly, where each of the sixty-six speakers had their own rooms, and, unfortunately, their own secretary.

I had only gone a few steps when a face under a bob of golden hair stuck around the next corner. The Etanela who had let me in must have heard my steps. She was wearing the kind of makeup many female working Etanela adopted, with tiny red dots above and below her eyes, her lips tinted deep purple against the faint blue of her face.

She came fully around the corner, putting away a tube of lipstick, and I stopped dead, my mind whirling. Something about her movement looked suddenly familiar, as if I knew her from somewhere, but I couldn't place it.

"Anything I can help you with?" she asked. "Are you finished with your interview? I'll just pop in and see what the Speaker—" Her hands clasped together in front of her, each massaging the other.

She must have seen something. She couldn't have killed him.

I interrupted her flow of words. "Ah, no. We're not done yet." What if...? "You haven't seen anyone come past, have you? Perhaps with a piece of paper?"

The secretary considered me, looking down from shoulders and head above me. Her eyes were watery, and still puffy from sleep. They would have been comically large on one of my species, but in her faintly blue, freckled face, they only looked earnest. "I haven't, but I got here just before you. You're the Speaker's first appointment." She shrugged. "He works odd hours. Sometimes early in the morning, sometimes late at night."

So whoever had killed him had left with the list just in time. I still needed to clear the Society from this mess, and somehow keep the Imperium guard from arresting me once this secretary figured out I'd been having an interview with a deceased speaker.

Perhaps a little misdirection. "The...the Speaker asked if he had another five minutes in his schedule." I shrugged. "He seems to have lost some information necessary to my presentation." I tried to keep my face neutral.

"Just a moment. I'll check." She sniffed, then ducked back around the corner, presumably to her desk. I let out a slow breath, trying to keep my hands from shaking.

In the few moments available, I focused on the

fading musical traces of the paper's thief. Whatever happened had been very recent, or I wouldn't have been able to still hear the notes. It went right by her desk, and unless I wanted to run past and alert everyone to the body, the musical trail would fade away before I could follow it. The way the music was dropping notes into inaudibility, it wouldn't be long until it was impossible to track.

The secretary popped around the corner again, her hands tracing elegant paths through the air. "He can spare another five minutes. I'll come tell you when the time is up."

She looks tired—must have been late coming in this morning. That will only make her feel worse when she finds the body.

"That will do nicely. I'll let him know," I said as I backed away, then threw a glance down at the chronograph. A few more minutes to search. Once I left, the Speaker's cooling body would not stay secret long. My only chance was to find a clue inside the room.

I paused at the door to make sure the secretary wasn't watching, then closed my eyes, separating out the bubbly, anxious music that defined her person from the rest of the Symphony of Healing.

Taking notes from my being, mimicking her chords and melodies, I tied them to a note keyed to the House of Potential. An aura of white and brown grew around me, visible only to maji—the physical results of changing the Symphony. I pressed my fingers on the doorframe, and the aura transferred to that spot. The new construct—a System—would send me an alerting tone if the secretary came down the corridor. Losing a few of my notes was worth the extra warning.

Inside the study, I closed the door, frowned at Speaker Thurapo's body, and scanned the room. The desk was the only other place to look, and the fading music pointed in that direction, though it was nearly inaudible.

The Speaker brought the paper from his desk. Why? To give to the killer?

I positioned myself where Speaker Thurapo would have sat, though my legs dangled as if I were a toddler, and spread one hand across the writing mat on the desk. It was leather, dyed green, with filigree around the edges. The Symphony of Healing held a last leitmotif woven through the writing mat, swirls of notes corresponding to the swirls of writing. The source of the paper's trail was here, maybe copied from another place. I only had a few more moments before it faded completely.

I closed my eyes, tracing the most recent indentations in the mat with a finger as I followed the music along a measure. I could *almost* make out what was written. It was a list of some sort, with names and...titles? Translating notes of the Symphony into writing was not something I had done before, and I hoped the tactile input from my finger would help me decipher the script.

My eyes flew open and the Symphony left me in a crash of noise. I was tracing my own name.

My finger continued its path, unaided now by the music in the back of my head. It would be even harder to catch hold of that particular sequence of notes before it disappeared. The Symphony did not like maji fiddling with it overly much.

Mandamon Feldo – Investigator

Why would this contain the name the Society used for my combination of houses? Only a member should know of them. I traced the next line, now more familiar with the indentations.

Tethan – Overwhelm

The name was vaguely familiar—another member who worked in chemistry, I believed—and I felt farther down.

Timpomitnob Gompt, Watcher – Archeologist

It was the name of my friend and colleague, working on the System Beast project. The little prototype was modeled after her. That meant the next line was probably...

Kratithakanipouliteka – Engineer

Yes, Kratitha, our project team's third member. It was conceivable the Speaker had all our names, likely even, as I had been scheduled to speak with him. But why and how were our Society titles included? What had this Tethan to do with it? The list went on.

Plithin A'Tyf – Psychiatrist

I knew him socially, a boorish Lobath.

There was one more indentation I could make out, below Plithin's name.

Moortlin – Biologist

No, this was no list of appointments. This was a list of the members of the Society of Two Houses with our internal titles, which no one outside our group should have. My heart sped at the implication. *The Speaker is not a majus, thus not a member of the Society. How did he get this? Someone else knows, but* what *do they know?*

I knew exactly who I needed to see.

Moortlin wouldn't like this. The Benish was paranoid about anything hinting at the Society's existence. Could I get proof for them?

I ran a hand over the desk drawers to search for paper to make a copy of the names, but a sustained tone rang in the back of my mind, and I held my chronograph to eye level. My time was up.

I sprang from behind the desk, grabbing my prototype model and then the extra chair as I went. The Symphony of Potential's beat grew louder as I dragged the legs across the rug beside Thurapo's corpse, creating friction. I flung open the door, stepping out into the surprised secretary's path, and left the chair teetering behind me, grabbing notes from my being and sliding them between measures in the music. I redirected the energy of friction and the movement of the falling chair into slightly different rhythms.

The door banged shut behind me, covering the noise the chair made as it reversed direction and hit the handle. "Just in time." I smiled at the secretary. "Thank you so much for coming to get me. The Speaker asked not to be disturbed for a few minutes, to write up a report."

I listened as I babbled, hearing the syncopation of the beat as the chair fell slowly, then stopped, fell *up*, and wedged under the door handle. That should keep prying eyes away for a short time.

"That is no problem at all," the secretary said. She flashed me a wide smile—she seemed more composed than she had been before, and I attempted to stretch my face into the same expression. "I was going to pop out for some tea anyway, to wake me up." She matched pace with me as we walked down the hall, away from the bloody mess in that room. My mind raced in the silence.

Just leave it alone. It's to your advantage. But no, I couldn't stop myself from asking the question.

"I...thought he had another appointment?" The secretary had checked his schedule.

"Oh...no." The Etanela's face creased in confusion for a moment, then cleared. "The Speaker is very busy, but it's not all meetings, naturally."

"I see," I said, trying to keep the anxiety from my face. We reached a branch in the corridor, and I listened for any hint of the musical trail I was seeking. It was gone, the music erased by new actions. "Well, enjoy your tea."

The secretary nodded and turned in the other direction. I picked up my pace. I would surely be implicated in this murder, once someone found the body. With the Society involved, I could not go to the Imperium guard. Fortunately, the Society had a lot of practice cleaning up embarrassing messes. Was it possible to fix this before the secretary returned from her tea?

* * *

The Spire of the Maji was a good few minutes' walk from the Dome of the Assembly, but my feet ate up the cobbles. I barely looked at the people I passed. Any of them could be the killer, and I had to work quickly. I was used to the alleys of the Imperium, the largest city and capital of the Nether, even if I didn't live here.

I circled one of the immense crystal columns—reaching higher than I could see—that dotted the enclosed, planet-sized interior of the Nether. This was the central hub for the ten species of the Great Assembly, rather than a homeworld, which meant there was a lot of traffic, with representation from every species. It also meant my list of suspects could have been quite long. However, it was reduced to those who knew about the Society of Two Houses—a very small number.

Inside the Spire, I passed the chamber of the Council of the Maji. The Council wasn't in session at this hour of the morning, but the one member who knew about the Society was nearby. I found Moortlin in their lab three levels higher in the Spire.

"Mandamon, hm, come in. None have followed this one, yes?" I shook my head at the question my mentor had asked every time I visited them in the Imperium over the last two cycles. Moortlin's paranoia was as healthy as ever.

Councilor Moortlin stepped away from their current project—a hybrid species of sticky trap tulip, meant to reduce the scritling population in the lower levels of the Spire. They were getting into the flour stores. "Then what is this one's, hm, question?"

The Benish was old, though how old they'd never shared. All I could do was compare with the others of their species I had seen. Moortlin's rough skin was no longer continuous, but peeling in fine strips, lighter patches showing beneath the walnut-colored exterior. Their unblinking yellow eyes stared into me.

"I have some unsettling news," I said, though my shaking hands and the sweat running into my beard showed that was an understatement. Not all of it was from my pace getting here, and I took a moment to straighten my suit. I had worn my best one to see Speaker Thurapo.

"The request for an audience with the Assembly? This one did not get a, hm, time to present?"

I paused. My presentation was such a small part of this. The Society might be able to arrange another speaker to sponsor the System Beast project, but this murder had to be tied up in a neat knot before then.

"That isn't it," I said, "but no, I could not schedule an audience."

Moortlin cocked their bald head with a creak like a teak tree shifting in the wind.

"Speaker Thurapo is dead." I let out the revelation in a breath, but then held up both hands, warding off my mentor's questions. "That is still not the extent of things. I did a little...Investigation."

Moortlin's pupil-less eyes flashed at my phrasing—a sign of concern in Benish.

"The Speaker had a list of Society members' names—potentially all of them," I said. "I think whoever killed him took it."

Moortlin crossed to the door of his lab—quickly for one of their species, which meant an odd straight-legged gait, sounding like someone snapping kindling into pieces. They closed it with a *click*.

"*Killed* then not, hm, *died*? And how does this one know what was on the list if it was not there?"

"The...*incident* must have happened moments before I arrived," I said. "There was still fading music in the Symphonies of Healing and Potential directing me to where the list had been. I found indentations on the Speaker's writing pad." I pressed a shaking hand to my pants leg to still it.

"This one came here first, yes?" Moortlin questioned. "Not to the, hm, Effature's guard?"

"Of course." I was slightly offended my mentor didn't trust me to keep our organization secret, and tried to remember they had seen many more cycles than I had. "I couldn't have said much with the geas, could I? I knew you would want to know first." My mentor's paranoia when dealing with the Society knew no bounds—warranted, in this case. I had absorbed some of those fears in the last half cycle I had been a member.

"It is good this one did not," Moortlin said. "Not even the Effature could prevent, hm, retribution against Society members if certain actions were discovered. There are...costs to how the Society brings new opportunities and conveniences to the public." They shook their head to another chorus of creaks and cracks, and I felt more justified in not going to the authorities.

"The Great Assembly must be protected from, hm, dangers it does not realize. That task falls to the Society." Moortlin's eyes held me. "What of the body?"

That was the more immediate problem. "I barred the door to the room, but I don't know how long it will hold," I replied. "Speaker Thurapo's secretary was going out, but will break into the room eventually, and call the Imperium guard." The energy I put into the chair would keep it snug to the door for several minutes—maybe up to a full lightening. "We need to clean up the body."

"One will manage that task soon," Moortlin assured me. "The Speaker will be discovered to have had a natural, if sudden, hm, death. *After* this one left."

What then? A speaker of the Great Assembly was still dead, and there were only sixty-six speakers among billions of inhabitants of the ten homeworlds. It would cause an upset, though the Assembly had procedures to replace a speaker who suffered a sudden death.

But procedures would not extend my time available to find the killer. Moortlin was on the Council of the Maji and also the head of the Society of Two Houses, but even they had only so much power to impede an official investigation if foul play was suspected.

"Could the names this one found be, hm, coincidence?" Moortlin asked.

"No." I wished they could be, but five, or more, names were a pattern. "Our Society titles were listed as well. Whoever wrote the list knew details about us, or copied them from another source. Someone has gotten around the geas."

I had only been in the Society for a short time, though long enough to see why our methods had to be kept secret. Many would condemn how we achieved such a rapid pace of innovation. During my six months in the Society, albeit with some diligent searching, I learned of those experiments involving sentient beings—voluntary and not, and others that included stolen and sensitive materials. Moortlin did not give out information easily, and the geas kept us safe. If someone got around its security, half our protection was gone.

"Then the Speaker's killer knows of this group," Moortlin said. "If word gets to the rest of the Council and the Assembly, the Society's days will be, hm, numbered. One will not allow this. Aegrino will be the best choice for these ones to talk to. The Society's record keeper will arrange things."

Moortlin took a key from a pocket in their loose vest. Benish rarely wore pants, as they were much more resistant to cold than the other species, and had no genitals to hide away.

They locked their door and creaked back to the middle of the room. "Stand back. These ones will go there directly."

"By portal?" I asked, surprised. The nearest portal ground—the one I used for my usual commute—was outside the Spire, not more than a few minutes' walk. Making a portal outside designated grounds was illegal, for reasons of safety, and even the Society mostly followed that rule, save for transfer of materials that might generate too much notice.

"These ones do not need more, hm, eyes making connections, especially so soon after Thurapo's murder. This one knows the Spire portal ground activity is recorded." I looked down. I should have remembered that, but the events of the morning had rattled me more than I thought. "All travel can be reported to the

Council. Even though one is Head of Healing, one can, hm, only divert so much."

An oval of blackness rotated into being in the center of Moortlin's study, ringed by green and white—the colors of the Benish's two houses. I heard the music of the House of Healing changing, since I shared that house with my mentor. The melody of their lab in the Spire—tranquil phrases looping in repetitive chords like a chiming clock—mixed with the familiar melody of the mansion in Poler, all the way on the opposite corner of the Nether. The music there was in another key, slower tempo, and lower pitched, but the two phrases melded together as the portal formed.

Moortlin gestured for me to step into the blackness. They would be last through the portal, as it would close when they reached the other side.

As I exited the portal, the musk of Moortlin's study in the Society of Two Houses made me wrinkle my nose. I could see flakes of their skin dusting the floor around the place where the Benish usually stood behind their desk. Their species was not well-equipped to sit.

Moortlin followed my gaze as they exited and the portal closed in a splash of white and green. "It is nearly time for one to return to one's homeworld of Aben and bud. This life has been long, and one has, hm, seen much. Perhaps this breach of the Society is a sign."

I frowned at my mentor. "Don't say that," I said. I had worked under Moortlin for a little over two cycles, ever since my original mentor in the House of Potential passed away. Majus Abarham Garhuk had led me through apprenticeship, though I had been close to him since I was a child. I let the usual tug of emotion wash through me at the memory, and my right hand rose to finger the scar around my right eye. I had almost lost it in the accident. But now was not the time to wallow in

Abarham's death—even if it had caused me to become a member of the Society.

My breathing came easier with the great distance from the Imperium, and the murder, but the incessant beat of the chronograph in my vest pocket urged me to action. "How can Aegrino help us with the body?" Clearly, the Society's record keeper held a lot of information, but I hadn't known he also cleaned up the Society's messes.

Moortlin's yellow eyes flashed again, deep emotion from the Benish, then they turned for the door, which was closed and locked. They were not one to let others see what they did not wish revealed.

"Aegrino will likely be in the library. These ones must let the record keeper know of the breach, and the Speaker's, hm, death, of course," Moortlin said. I felt that was second in their thoughts, only relevant by the threat to the Society. I followed them down the carpeted hall, doors lining the walls.

Hallways branched off at intervals in the sprawling structure. The Society of Two Houses was a mansion in Poler, the city on the opposite side of the Nether from its capital, the Imperium—where the Effature, the Council, and the Great Assembly were all based. Without a portal made by a majus, it would take a very long time to traverse the distance between the two.

We passed members of the Society along the way, some familiar, and some not. Even though the murder pressed me onwards, I slowed and stared at a strange being strolling by. I knew the individual must be a Lobhl, though I had not seen one of their species until now. They had only joined the Great Assembly a cycle ago.

My eyes naturally fell away from the Lobhl's face and

down to their hands, which were extravagantly tattooed, with five fingers and two thumbs each. They gave me a quick twirl of their fingers in greeting and I waved back.

"Touching Digits is our newest member," Moortlin said. They must have heard the hesitation in my step. "One gave that one the geas not three days ago."

Down two more hallways and another three turns was the library, the repository of information the Society collected over the cycles and deemed too revealing to give to the larger maji community. It was put to better use furthering the Society's contributions to the Great Assembly.

Aegrino was the current record keeper, and the Etanela had been at the job for over twenty cycles, so I was told. There were still many secrets in this place, as Moortlin had only decided I could be trusted with the Society's existence after a cycle-and-a-half training under them.

Majus Aegrino Plumera Lunigi met us a few steps into the library. Aegrino was tall, even for an Etanela, reaching nearly half again my height, and I couldn't help but make comparisons to Speaker Thurapo. They might have been of an age, though Majus Aegrino had a mane of golden hair tied back in a severe bun, revealing the thin blueish planes of his face. His eyes were bright and large as his hands waved in the air. Something tugged at my thoughts, but his next words blew the feeling away like a cloud on a windy day.

"Moortlin, thank the Sea Mother you're here. I must speak with you. Something terrible has happened," Aegrino's ever-moving hands described fluid arcs by his sides, his words slurring together in his excitement.

"Another, hm, problem?" Moortlin rumbled. "Today seems a stimulating one."

"I was revising the list of Society members yesterday," Aegrino continued over Moortlin's words. "Adding our new members from the last half cycle—" Here a hand waved in my direction, "—and I left it on my desk for the night. When I came back this morning, it was gone."

I exchanged a look with my mentor. Moortlin's yellow eyes were flashing.

"Foolish of you," they chastised. "One has cautioned all the, hm, members of the Society of leaving important information where others can find it. This one knows better." Aegrino grimaced and waved an apologetic hand. Moortlin continued. "Nevertheless, this is not, hm, a new problem, but the same one of which these ones were to speak."

"Speaker Thurapo is dead," I told the record keeper. "He was to be our sponsor for the System Beast project, but when I got there, I found him on the floor of his room at the Dome with his throat cut." I drew in a breath, pushing up my glasses, which had slid down my nose again. "He had a list of the Society's members." Considering how closely we guarded that information, the list could only have come from Aegrino's desk. *Who had taken it?*

"Speaker Thurapo?" The majus blinked several times at me, fingers waving languidly. "Oh my. Oh Sea Mother. He spoke for my home district on Etan. I must tell my sister, if she doesn't already know. She...will be very upset." He searched around, as if one of the records would reverse my words, then spared a glance at Moortlin. "No, not now. Later, of course, after this is over." His eyes found me again. "Oh, but the list! You have it? Quickly, give it here." He made a pulling motion with both hands. "We are still in danger of others finding out—"

"It may be too late already," I broke in. Aegrino was normally a little scattered, but the news about the Speaker's death seemed to have hit him hard. "The list was stolen. I only know the Speaker had it by using my houses to track the paper's history. More importantly, we must clean up the body before the Imperium guard finds it."

Majus Aegrino paled to a light blue, then pivoted in place, gathering a few slips of paper and a quill. He crossed the room and slipped between two bookshelves. I heard rustling, as if he was searching for equipment. His disembodied head poked out over their tops. "I will handle it myself directly," he called back. "My sister is in the Imperium in any case."

"This one will not share any sensitive information, naturally," Moortlin cautioned, and Aegrino answered with a grunt. "Additionally, the Speaker's body must be found in, hm, natural death."

"There is a chair wedging the door closed from the inside," I added. "Symphony of Potential."

At least the geas will keep him from blabbing about the Society to his sister. I'd tested the limits when I was first inducted, which was how I knew of the further debilitating effects, past the distracting music. The geas was sometimes applied to family, so it was conceivable his sister was included, though usually it was only for those who lived at the mansion, and when absolutely necessary.

Aegrino nodded and his head disappeared as I turned to the councilor. Even if Aegrino concealed the murder, that left the list, and I had no idea where the culprit was.

I checked my chronograph. The secretary was surely back from her break. Would Aegrino be in time to stop her entering the room?

And what is it that feels wrong about this situation?

"What if the Society is revealed?" I asked Moortlin. "The geas will make us look guiltier if we cannot defend ourselves in court. Would the Council even let us rejoin the rest of the maji?" I tried to think of what raw material and equipment I had used. How much had we stolen? From where? At least I had not done experimentation on live subjects.

Councilor Moortlin regarded me for a moment, their eyes dulling, deep in thought. Maybe all the secrecy was based on their paranoia. Maybe losing the list was not so bad.

Don't delude yourself.

"This one has been with the Society for less than a cycle, Mandamon," Moortlin finally said. "One rarely shares the Society's secrets for, hm, many cycles more, but with this development, one judges it necessary for this one to know more of this group's, hm, history. These ones can spare a few minutes while Aegrino cleans up the Speaker's office—even with other pressing matters."

The Benish creaked, shifting from one gnarled foot the other, as if still unsure whether to let any more information go. Then they reached for the doorknob with a sound of snapping branches. As I followed them back into the corridor, I heard the *pop* of a portal opening. Aegrino was on his way.

"Does this one know how old one is?" Moortlin asked as we walked down the Society's halls.

I frowned, thrown by the question. I knew the Benish were long-lived beings, perhaps the longest lived of the ten species of the Assembly. They were secretive about how their kind reproduced and how their parents—progenitors—taught them.

How will this help me find the list?

"I do not, Councilor," I answered.

"One is nearing the three hundred and seventy second cycle of existence," Moortlin said. I must have stopped, because they did too, half-turning in my direction.

"It is long even for one's people." They brushed a flake of skin from their arm, revealing a lighter surface underneath—the Benish had a dense, hard flesh, more like aged wood than muscle and meat. "But one's time has been, hm, busy, keeping the Society a secret from the Assembly while promoting new technology and social change. Otherwise beings would live shorter, uglier lives."

They took a rasping step forward and I followed. "One has watched this one's progress for many cycles, even before this one's, hm, second house emerged. It was such a tragedy to hear of this one's mentor, and family—" They broke off abruptly as I stiffened. It was still a tender subject. "—but, hm, leaving that aside, this one's inventions were what first attracted one's attention."

My second house—Healing, like Moortlin—was only beginning to show when the Benish contacted me, a few days after the accident, my wounds still fresh. I had recently passed my test to graduate from apprentice to majus, and was flattered one of the Council thought so well of me. I'd assumed such a catastrophe would doom my chances of amounting to anything in the ranks of the maji.

However, the councilor urged me to downplay my second house so others would forget. They offered tips and training, helping me find my strengths in the House of Healing. Those ran to inert organic materials, and despite the name, actual healing was an effort for me.

We reached Moortlin's study and entered. The councilor glanced both ways down the hallway before shutting and locking the door.

"This one's inventions are the talk of the Society," Moortlin continued. I made some feeble protest, my mind straying to the cooling form of Speaker Thurapo, but the Benish spread a thick hand out in negation. "No, there is no reason for, hm, false modesty. This one will be a force in the maji for cycles to come."

Flattering, but how does this help me find the list? Yet Moortlin continued, as if we had all the time in the Nether.

"Mark these words. This one's work on replicating a picture over long distances was perhaps ahead of its time, but focusing harmonic resonances into physical form and recording changes to Systems can surely, hm, be used in a cycle or two, once the issues are resolved. Finally, there are the System Beasts."

"Those still need fine tuning, before the big presentation to the Assembly," I objected, "and really, it is a combined effort with Gompt and Kratitha. They have each done at least as much as I on the project, if not more." However I *was* proud of the automatons. They could be incredibly helpful assistants, once they were approved for sale.

"Yet the original idea was this one's." Moortlin gently poked me in the chest with one thick finger. "Such ingenuity is important to encourage and develop, and the Society is the best place to, hm, do so."

I stared at Moortlin, realizing the Benish was much more worried than I had previously thought.

"This one asked about the repercussions of the Society becoming widely known. One has witnessed this firsthand," Moortlin said. "In the past, the Society was shut down and its members prosecuted."

My face must have reflected my astonishment. I pushed my glasses back up my nose. "Shut down? When? How? What happened to the two-house maji?" I smoothed my beard as my stomach tried to turn a flip. "It can't have been recently. Majus I'Ban's work with visual communication was made public ten cycles ago, and Majus' Juut, Thinker's work with pistols was twenty cycles before that."

"Precisely the issue," Moortlin answered. "This one has lived in a privileged time for the, hm, Society. One has kept our members safe, with plenty of resources. Everyone knows the maji provide new scientific advancement, and, hm, no longer question how such technological leaps arise. The Society becomes complacent." Moortlin's eyes flickered and they stumped to their desk, rooting through a stack of papers nearly the height of their head. Their motions were sharp, like twigs popping in a fire.

They're...furious. I'd never seen the Benish truly angry. They shoved papers aside as they searched, quicker than I'd ever seen them move. The controlled power of their movements frightened me more than their revelation of the prosecution of Society members.

Moortlin pulled a sheaf of papers out, cocked their head, and put them aside. "When one was very young—perhaps, hm, 630 A.A.W.—one was apprenticeship, ready to become a majus." They pulled aside another section of the stack. "The Society then was run by Councilor Fortilath, head of the House of Communication, though that was, hm, not revealed until several cycles after the Society was shuttered. The geas was not in effect, then."

That's over three hundred and twenty cycles ago!

"Did one of the members let the secret out?" I asked.

Moortlin shook their head and thrust a sheaf of paper at me—very old, and with writing scribbled in the margins.

Society of war maji shut down!

It has come to the attention of the Assembly of Species, the Council of the Maji, and the Effature, that the clan of maji named the 'Society of Two Houses' has been practicing forbidden energies of war, for the express purpose of fomenting outrage and rebellion within the eight homeworlds of the Great Assembly. Not since the Aridori war of old has such an affront to the sovereignty of the Assembly been perpetrated. These maji, even more powerful in their sound magics than the rest of the maji, have used live subjects to research ways to incapacitate armies, reduce buildings to rubble, and connect portals in tandem in order to transit from homeworld to homeworld in the blink of an eye! Fortunately, the suspected maji were discovered by a group of Kirian private agents before any further damage was done. Several have been sent to Gloomlight Prison, and their place of work torn down.

I handed the page back with a frown.

"The facts are distorted," Moortlin said, their eyes' intense glow dimming along with their anger. "The Society was, hm, researching defenses against inter-homeworld conflict, brought on by hostilities between the Etanela and the Festuour over trading rights for a type of, hm, luxury fabric."

"The methods for discovering defenses required, hm, *volunteers* from the war to test said defenses. Councilor Fortilath was caught on the battlefield by that one's own people. The public feared the Society would, hm, pull down their homes and take them as test subjects. Completely unfounded, as the two-house maji were, hm, trying to protect others."

"We're not in a war now," I said. "People would act differently."

"And what would they say if information was shared about this one's, hm, device focusing sonic energy?" Moortlin asked.

Is that a threat? Or merely to remind me I'm complicit as well? As if I needed another reminder.

"After the accident, I stopped working on sonics immediately," I said, then swallowed. My hands were in fists at my sides. I clenched them to keep from touching the scar on my face. The accident was not my fault. *It wasn't.* I'd spent the last two cycles wrestling with myself over it. I thought I had gotten rid of these feelings of guilt, but Moortlin's casual reference brought them back full-fold.

"That is of little import." Moortlin gestured back to the pile of papers with one hand. "The Society of Two Houses has formed, and, hm, been destroyed, at least four separate times since the Aridori war. Possibly more. Each time, fifty or sixty cycles must pass before the Assembly and the Council forgets the 'danger' and the Society can reform. Always, much knowledge is lost—knowledge that, hm, should be used to help the species of the Great Assembly."

Moortlin paced the room, creaking like branches in a storm. "This is why a member of the Society—the head, preferably—is also a member of the Council of the Maji, by election or, hm, trickery. One has been on the Council twice over the course of one's life." Moortlin looked at me. "One will do whatever is necessary to keep the Society from the notice of the other maji."

What is Moortlin capable of? The Benish had lived a long time and was crafty. Could this all be a sham? Could Moortlin themself have killed the Speaker and taken the list? Then why go through this ruse of alerting Aegrino? Were they *that* paranoid?

I shook my head. I'd worked with them closely for two cycles, and my instincts said Moortlin couldn't be involved.

"What if we brought the matter to the Effature privately?" I asked. "He's a reasonable man—he would surely see our side."

Moortlin laughed—a mirthless bark. He gestured to me. "This one is still young. One has known the Nether's caretaker far longer, enough to know the Effature is, hm...chameleonic, changing with the times." Moortlin paused, then cocked their head again. "Nevertheless, it would not help. The Effature is under the same geas as the Society."

I goggled. "The Effature knows?" The self-styled caretaker of the Nether influenced much of the finance, business, and lawmaking between the Imperium and the other cities in the Nether. He presided over the Great Assembly, though only rarely lent his voice to the debate.

"A directive from the post of the Effature originally began the Society," Moortlin said. "Has this one heard of maji born to three houses?"

My face certainly showed my confusion. That was a night-tale, told by nursemaids to children.

"It is no made up story. The Society keeps records on such rare, hm, cases." Moortlin turned to another corner of their desk, where a neat stack of papers sat under an enormous volume of plant species native to the Nether. "They are very, very rare. Rarer than, hm, two-house maji are to one-house maji. Those who are born show symptoms immediately, so in tune with the Symphony are they. None with the potential ever survived past two cycles of age, in any records one has discovered," their pupil-less eyes fixed me in place, "and which one has concealed from the Council." They patted the volume of botany protectively. "The overload of so much of the Symphony causes madness, and eventually death. This one knows the, hm, instability of some of the two-house members."

I hesitated, then nodded. Living in the mansion afforded an easy opportunity to see that many two-house maji were eccentric at best. Moortlin's paranoia was a prime example. Many of us, myself included, sometimes struggled to connect with others.

"The original directive was for those with two houses to protect against the potential threat of those with access to three houses," Moortlin said.

"That makes no sense," I said. "If none with the ability to hear three Symphonies live to use such abilities, then why is it a problem?" I tried to imagine hearing three of the aspects of the Grand Symphony. The combinations multiplied exponentially. *They could change half the music of the universe at will.*

"One sees the risk is understood," Moortlin said. "No such beings live here, but what if another civilization were to find the Nether, as the Lobhl did a few cycles ago? What if they have, hm, a militarized maji corps, and have harnessed those with three houses? The Great Assembly frowns on martial use of the Symphony. And so, the Society must guard against such an incursion. This group's other inventions are a fortunate offshoot of the core directive."

What other subjects were researched behind closed doors, and what forbidden resources did they use, even past those practices I had already discovered? I had been caught up in the rush of new scientific study, and meeting Gompt and Kratitha—realizing there were others like me who yearned for more knowledge than available within the Great Assembly of Species. No doubt it was precisely what Moortlin intended, to keep new members busy.

They crossed close enough I could smell the musty resin of their flesh. "There are much worse things out there, hm, in the wide universe," the Benish said. "Which ones are to say the next species contacting the Nether will be benevolent?" They shook their head and I winced at the crackling sound. "The Society of Two Houses is necessary as a first, but, hm, secret line of defense against the unknowns of the universe. It cannot be shut down without great loss of knowledge. It leaves the Great Assembly undefended until its resurrection."

They turned away, making their stiff-legged stride across their study, pacing once more. "This one is the Investigator one most trusts, though this one is new to the Society."

Moortlin stopped before me. "One is known far too well in the Assembly. One's placement on the Council of the Maji means one's moves are, hm, tracked closer than one would like."

They took in a deep breath, their chest creaking with the effort. "Mandamon, investigate this missing list of Society members. While Aegrino, hm, cleans up the murder, this one must find who took the list as quickly as this one can. Keep the Society alive."

"What about the System Beast project?" I protested.

Moortlin raised their hands to stop me. "It will wait a few days if needed. There is no other choice. Include this one's colleagues, but this is, hm, not to go farther that this group's small circle."

They breathed out, a gust of exhalation like the groan of a great tree. "One must return to Aben soon. The time to find a group to plant with is coming. One's memories will be passed down to the next generation of Benish, but one's work with the Society?" Their eyes dimmed. "It must remain with the two-house maji. This one—" they poked my chest again, "—is the best choice. Solve this mystery and keep the Society active for another hundred cycles."

I rocked back at the enormity of the task Moortlin had just entrusted me with. *Surely there are others better suited?*

"I will figure out who took the list, Moortlin," I said. I clenched my hands, pushing away memories of my first mentor, now dead. If the Society was closed down, I had nowhere else to go—my own actions had guaranteed that.

PART TWO

The Mansion

- The Society, it has been my home for over forty cycles, accepting me when the maji ridiculed my ideas about the new chemical substances I have devised. Altering the chemicals the brain produces can be dangerous, yes, but could also prove invaluable to help those with social and behavioral differences such as myself. The other two-house maji, they helped push my discoveries into the main body of majus work, but I fear my ideas will never be fully utilized without backing from the Council, and that would require revelation of my situation in the Society.

Personal Journal of Tethan, Sathssn majus of the Houses of Strength and Power, titled "Overwhelm."

Thoughts of undiscovered species of martial beings with maji in chains followed me as I walked down the corridors of the mansion in Poler. Moortlin was paranoid, but I suspected they were also correct to worry about the fate of the Society. They could not have been involved in the murder—not with such passion for two-house maji, and for so many cycles. The original Society even had a blessing from the Effature at the time, hundreds of cycles ago.

I thought back on my twenty-and-six cycles in the Nether. Moortlin had lived for nearly fifteen times that long. What secrets would the Benish take with them when they returned to their homeworld?

My feet led me to the lower floors of the mansion. As I had not designed my inventions alone, so I could not solve this mystery alone. I had not met many Society members—by nature, we were secretive and antisocial—

but the two I worked with were skilled, intelligent, and I trusted them. Their fortunes were bound up in the success of the System Beast project, which was threatened by Speaker Thurapo's death. Maybe the others could help me discover who killed him, and who had the list of Society names.

I could hear Gompt and Kratitha arguing before I entered the laboratory. I couldn't leave those two alone for even one lightening of the Nether's walls before they were off again, debating the best method of calculating efficiency. They shared the ability to hear the Symphony of Grace, and both had opinions on the best way to reduce the effort required to power the System Beasts.

We shared a spacious area in the Society mansion, cluttered by the results of our work. Kratitha was the worst, for she flitted from project to project even faster than she spoke. Gompt was slower, more deliberate, but she was as young as the rest of us, and still prone to flights of fancy. I preferred to at least get a prototype working before I moved to a new project, but I was certainly guilty of abandoning my share.

I edged past a massive construct of pipes and hoses—a failed attempt to harness performed music and compare it with the Symphony—and around stacks of books to arrive at the heart of our workshop. I was surrounded by our many iterations of System Beast design, each crafted in a different form of creature from across the Nether and the ten homeworlds.

"—find the screw for my glasses, Kratitha?" Gompt was asking. "I've been trying to fix the actuator on the new prototype without them for half a lightening." The Festuour was gesturing expansively with one furry arm, and I stepped back to avoid being hit.

"Speaker Thurapo is—" I began, but Kratitha cut me off.

"Yes, yes, found screw and fixed them just now, but had idea," she chirruped. Her wings were a blur and she held her small body at table height, peering through Gompt's glasses first with one, then another section of her compound eyes. "Need to see windings on motor. Too many for magnetic ratio. Glasses magnification most helpful. Though could add another lens to glasses to account for distribution in Pixie focal lengths."

"I calculated the ratio yesterday," Gompt said. "We wound it too tightly before. Take off six rotations and it should work. And calm down—your wings are going faster than I've even seen. I swear, you're jumpier than a pelt flea on fire today."

"The Speaker is—" my teeth clicked together as the Pixie spoke over me.

"One moment. Done!" Kratitha looked up in triumph. "Mandamon. Appointment with Speaker was successful? Was anticipating you back sooner." She buzzed to another table, half walking, half flying. "See the new motion control for the System Beast? We think it may provide better autonomy when—"

I barely got my mouth open this time.

"When it has to switch interaction targets," Gompt interrupted. "I also thought it would fit in the casing better and provide better control." She followed the Pixie a few steps. "Kratitha, my glasses, remember?"

Kratitha held the lenses in front of her multifaceted eyes once more, then gave them absently to the Festuour before peering into the interior of our largest prototype System Beast, created in the shape of a Kirian Ethulina pullbeast.

Gompt thrust her glasses back on her snout, blinking through them with bright blue eyes. They were slightly askew from Kratitha's ministrations, and Gompt tried to straighten the frame. "Now how did the interview go? Did Speaker Thurapo agree? By what date do we need this ready?" She thumped the casing on the Ethulina, causing Kratitha to jump in surprise. Her head had nearly been enclosed in the pullbeast's interior. "Kratitha, did you do something to my glasses? They work...better."

"Ground left lens slightly," Kratitha said. "Focus was off. Also adjusted focal length with—"

I drew a deep breath, then shouted, "Speaker Thurapo is dead!"

There was silence, as both Gompt and Kratitha stared at me, open-mouthed.

I took the model Festuour from my vest pocket. It was the first working System Beast Gompt had made. She'd come straight to the maji from her friend group on Festuour, at an early age. They had moved with her to the Imperium, but she still didn't get to see them often. I think the model may have been a subconscious attempt to give her another of her species she could relate to. The three of us had grown closer since then.

I handed the model back to Gompt.

"Worse than that, the Speaker held a list of members of the Society. We could be shut down if the Great Assembly finds out about us and our...resource acquisition." I frowned. "Or some of the experiments other members have performed."

"Who would kill Speaker Thurapo?" Kratitha asked. Her wings were buzzing in agitation—an emotion I could easily agree with. "Must have just happened."

"That's what I'm trying to discover," I said, and briefly described the scene I found in the Speaker's study, the missing list, and how I left his body.

"What is Moortlin doing about this?" Gompt asked.

I drew another breath. "They have tasked me with finding the killer and returning the list of names. They said they were too well known to do it, and you know how paranoid they are." I waved a hand in exasperation. "They didn't want to tell anyone else about the problem."

"Well, they are head of House of Healing," Kratitha said. She tapped a wrench into one blueish hand. "When do we start?"

"Right now." I nodded to the Pixie. She was a rarity among the small beings, as most Pixies belonged to the warrior class. The other species looked down upon them as being less intelligent. Kratitha was one of the declining scientist class, and made sure others knew it. The slow death of her class resulted from some world war fifty-odd cycles ago—a lifetime for the short-lived species.

"Aegrino is cleaning up the mess in the Speaker's study," I began, "but Moortlin wants me to search out the killer."

"Because you are Investigator, yes yes." Kratitha was nodding along.

Gompt had one furry finger raised, mouth open, as if about to make the same point. She glared at the Pixie.

"We must start at the beginning then." Gompt said. "Why was the Speaker killed? Who has cause to know about the Society? Who benefits from giving away the list of members? Are they being paid by someone, or working for themselves?"

I didn't miss Gompt's accusation, and neither did Kratitha. "Assume two-house member was paid to give it away?" she asked.

"Or was blackmailed. Who else would even have known, with our enforced silence?" Gompt replied.

"How would they get around the geas? That jingle is enough to drive anyone mad—even before it incapacitated them—if they tried to bypass it to show off a list of Society names."

Kratitha's hands clasped tightly together. "Might be circumvented. Two-house maji have many resources." She scuttled to the prototype, absently checking torque on the System Beast's bolts.

I watched her, tugging my beard in thought. The Ethulina pullbeast was a work of art. We'd formed the mane of crested feathers from crystal slivers that reflected light, and the claw-hooves were of solid steel, etched with filigree. Kratitha and Gompt had spent a ten-day attaching wooden representations of the scales along its body, hiding the service hatches—one of which the Pixie had open now. She flipped several switches and the pullbeast raised one forehoof, which split into separate digits. Even though the System Beast imitated a draft animal, we had increased its dexterity to allow for grasping and holding.

The creature was starting to look as impressive as we first imagined, and its mannerisms were almost entirely lifelike, with the latest adjustments to the gearing ratios. The model I would have shown the Speaker was a toy compared with our masterpiece. We had to bring this to the Assembly, and demonstrate how the System Beast project could help our culture. They could be used as servants, and recorders, but also as a way for physical invalids to interact with the rest of the Nether. Our customers would think of many more uses once our creations were public.

That meant we had to find the killer, and the list.

"The geas hasn't failed in nearly three hundred cycles, to hear Moortlin talk," I said. "I'm sure they've tested it extensively." *What am I missing?* "Did someone find the list by accident?"

"And give it to the Speaker? And then kill him?" Gompt asked. "Why? The list would be meaningless to one who doesn't know what the Society is—just a list of names with words after them."

"Important point," Kratitha said.

"So only a Society member would know what the list meant, but would have to get around the geas to give it to the Speaker," I said. "Someone outside wouldn't have access to the list, but would have no trouble transporting it to the Speaker. I still don't see the motive to kill him."

"You didn't send any information on ahead of your appointment, did you?" Gompt asked. "The list could have been stuck to another page like a suckerfish on a whale."

"Now you think *I* did it?" I raised my eyebrows at the Festuour.

Kratitha tsked from where she was studying a selection of springs. "Not suspecting. Could have been an unfortunate accident. Maybe no one guilty. Or could have been coercion. Ah!" She picked a coil of wire out and fluttered back to the prototype, fitting it in the head cavity. "Might fix the head stutter issue."

Gompt's attention was diverted. "Does it match the calculations on the harmonics in the House of Grace?" she asked. "I've been looking for the right tension constant for three days."

"If we could attend to the murder and the Society being shut down?" I suggested. Gompt and Kratitha both turned to me, looking chagrined. "I sent the proposal to the Speaker myself last ten-day. There were no extra papers included. Even if we limit our search to Society members, and I think that's a better guess, we can't just ask everyone whether they're plotting to shut us down."

The two considered, and I looked around the workshop for inspiration. The numerous small automatons—previous attempts at System Beasts, on a lesser scale—stared back. The full-size prototype was the first of its kind. Others had exposed gearing, or no coverings at all. The skeletal face of a rodent-shaped beast peered at me from one shelf, its lidless eyes frozen in a glassy stare. Its beat in the Symphony of Potential was mechanical, a representation of the System's artificial construct. "Is there a way to use the prototypes to gather information?" I asked.

Gompt followed my gaze. "I suppose I could alter the gearing in some of the old ones to record waveforms, and leave them around the mansion," she said. "We might happen on important information."

"Too long," Kratitha argued. "Need quick answer, before killer gets too far with list." She waved her wrench vaguely, taking in the Nether as a whole.

"I can adjust a few," Gompt protested. She held up the model I'd taken to the Speaker's office this morning. The little figure held a tiny drum, which disguised a wax cylinder, where the figure could inscribe sums. "I can change the gearing to make it write sound waves rather than mathematical figures."

Kratitha, drawn as ever by a challenge, drifted forward. "Will have to account for sound wave distortion," she said. "House of Grace can help in cutting out noise, but will need to tune System powering it."

"The smaller scale can be used to filter the lower register," Gompt said, lifting the figure out of the Pixie's grasping fingers. "There are a few others I can adjust the same way."

"New algorithm must be altered for differences in size and shape—" Kratitha was already searching the standing, half-disassembled prototypes. "Ah. This one." She pointed to a System Beast in the form of a sticky lizard, with adhesive feet made to climb walls. It was missing its tail and lower jaw, but it carried a similar wax cylinder on its back, a stylus positioned nearby. We had played with replicating animal sounds with this one. It would work even better than the one Gompt held.

"This will require what, two or three lightenings to adjust?" I asked. "Moortlin wants this tied up as quickly as possible—today, if we can."

"If we get the gearing right the first time," Gompt said. She played with her glasses thoughtfully. "What do you think, Kratitha?"

"Two lightenings, maximum," Kratitha said, still tapping sections of the lizard. "Can finish while you investigate Society members." She looked back at us, compound eyes reflecting many facets of the room. "Go, go. Will work here. Talk to others to save time."

"I guess that's our dismissal," I told Gompt. In truth, I was having trouble keeping my hand from drifting to my chronograph. I wondered if Aegrino had intercepted Speaker Thurapo's secretary in time. *Or did she find the body?*

"Remember to account for the waveform distribution of the System Beast so we don't pick up any echoes this time," Gompt called as I propelled her out with a hand on her furry arm. Kratitha waved a hand in acknowledgement.

We strolled out of the workshop, picking a direction in the mansion largely by happenstance. We had only gotten a few paces down the hall before Gompt began a rumbling hum, thinking.

"You're right. We can't ask every member of the Society where they've been and what their motivations are."

"I don't even *know* half the members," I said. "You've been here longer than me."

"Only by a few ten-days," Gompt replied. "Kratitha was here several months before me, but I doubt she's gone to any lengths to meet others. Keeps her head down lower than a racing canis on the scent."

I added combinations in my head. "Six houses, fifteen combinations of two-house member abilities—"

"Though not all equally represented," Gompt added.

"True, but with a hundred and some members in the Society, there must be at least two or three of each type. Could a specific combination affect the geas?"

"Maybe," Gompt adjusted the bandolier that held her favorite selection of tools. Festuour liked accessories— hats, glasses, scarves, belts, and bandoliers—more than clothes. There was little point with all that fur. "But I'm nigh certain I've heard Moortlin say the geas was built up from all six houses. Hard for one majus to get around that."

"So you're saying it could be more than one?" I wasn't ready to dig a conspiracy out of a secret society. That felt like one too many layers.

Gompt waggled a three-fingered paw as we turned into the next hallway, where some of the Society's clinical studies took place. "Possible, but I doubt it. What about the section of the list you found? Whose names were on it? They might be ones the Speaker was paying more attention to."

In the interest of time, it was a good place to start. I thought back. "The three of us," I began. "That would be the Houses of Potential and Healing for me, and Potential and Grace for you—"

"And Kratitha would be Grace and Power." Gompt was nodding along.

"Moortlin was on the list as well, and they're a Biologist—Houses of Strength and Healing." *That's odd.* "In fact, I'm surprised Moortlin was not more concerned about their name getting out, considering their place on the Council."

"I'm sure they've got the politics of this all tied up. Have you ever heard Moortlin sound unsure about anything?" Gompt peered at me over her spectacles. "How inept would the Council be to let a scandal take down its members? Anyway, as secretive as the friendless old root is, I can't believe they had anything to do with this. What about the other names?"

"If we discount us and the Benish..." I searched through my hazy memory. Both names had been familiar. "One was Tethan, of the Houses of Strength and Power."

"So an Overwhelm," Gompt said. We walked up a staircase, passing a Lobath talking with another Festuour in hushed tones. Gompt watched the one of her species as we passed, but the Festuour didn't notice her.

"What are their strengths?" I asked. I hadn't seen an Overwhelm in action.

"Strength and Power give some ability to push others to do what they want, and to pry objects apart into components," Gompt said. "If anyone could take apart the geas, an Overwhelm could. Sounds fishy to me."

I had to admit my friend was right, but my memory of Tethan was of a small, frail Sathssn. "Have you seen her recently?"

Gompt shrugged. "I went up to her room to ask her a question once about the System Beasts responding to chemical signals."

"I doubt she's murdered more than a hot meal in cycles," I said.

"Still prudent to follow every lead, and this is all we have right now," Gompt said. The maji who lived here would have apartments in their primary House back in the Imperium, but I had found most in the Society preferred the obscurity of Poler, desiring to follow their own studies without interruption, or any distracting ethical questions.

We found Tethan on the third level, tucked into a corner of the mansion. The sprawling house was big enough for new members to get lost in. I'd lost my way frequently in my first few ten-days.

I knocked on the red painted door of the majus' room. Gompt and I traded glances at the chorus of thumps and complaints coming from inside. There was another clatter, as if a stack of plates had fallen to the floor.

"Maybe later?" Gompt suggested, and I almost stepped away when the doorknob rattled.

The red painted wood opened a crack and a slitted red and yellow eye, surrounded by gray-green scales peeked out.

"Yes? You are here about the pipes?"

"Ah—Majus Tethan?" I asked, somewhat at a loss.

"Yes. That is me. I have been sending messages about the pipes for ten-days now. You, come in."

The door rattled closed, and Gompt frowned at the sounds of metal latches being unfastened. Then the door opened again, showing an ancient Sathssn, gray of scale and shaky, with white wisps of hair floating around her head. I was nearly as surprised at her age as I was at the lack of coverings. Tethan wore no cowl, had on short sleeves, and her tunic was dark blue—something I had never seen on a Sathssn.

"I thought they all wore black?" Gompt whispered. Tethan peered at us as if she had heard something, then shook her head and gestured with a scaled hand for us to come in. A short black skirt covered the majus only halfway down her legs, and below she wore open sandals rather than the more common enclosed boots.

We followed the old Sathssn inside and Tethan hobbled around us to close and latch the door again.

"Now, my pipes, they have been squeaking for months, but Moortlin refuses to send anyone up here." Tethan shuffled around to look at us, then away, leading us farther into the apartment. "At least until now."

The room was uncomfortably warm, and I pulled at the collar of my shirt as Gompt opened her mouth in a pant. Books were stacked everywhere, with trinkets, statues, and little plates piled on top as if the books were plinths. It was a collection of plates that had tumbled to the floor by the door.

Something squawked by my foot and I hastily looked down.

"Don't worry about Scampers. Him, he complains all the time," Tethan said. A scaled creature with six legs rubbed against me, leaving a white smear on my best pants. "Especially right now, as he is molting."

I shook off the thing and glared at Gompt, whose tongue lolled in silent Festuour laughter.

"The sound, it is right back here." Tethan waved a wizened arm, and I could barely stop myself from staring at the loose scaly skin.

I don't think I've ever seen—or want to see again—so much bare Sathssn flesh.

She knocked at a wall and I jumped at a chittering whine that grew louder, vanishing to a shriek. It sounded almost organic, but I had heard all sorts of sounds from these old walls.

"We—we wanted to ask a few questions," I attempted, but Tethan was shuffling along, not paying any attention.

"The pipes, they run along here." She traced a finger along the wall. "Nothing in the Symphony of Strength, but me, I hear a repeating arpeggio in the melody of Power." She looked to me and I looked to Gompt, who shrugged—neither of us could hear the House of Power.

"What about the House of Potential?" I suggested. There might be an overlap. Gompt sighed, but her blue eyes took on a faraway look, even as I tuned into the music that echoed though my head.

"Yes, I hear it," I said. "There's a chord progression like something—"

"Something blocked. Energy is building," Gompt said.

I nodded. The rhythm was natural, like that of a wind tunnel. What did those pipes transmit? Not fluid. Maybe they heated the upstairs. If so, then Tethan must have requested her vents opened all the way for the apartment to be so warm.

Gompt walked down the hall, knocking on the wall. I took the chance to corner the old majus.

"What do you work on?" I asked.

"Oh this and that," Tethan shrugged. "Now, not so much as before. But twenty cycles past, I was making some of the best psychotropic chemicals available. The remedies, the Assembly decided they were too dangerous, even for those who needed them, so here I sit." She spread scaled hands to the messy apartment.

Mind altering chemicals? My thoughts raced. Like something that could make a speaker cut his own throat? "Can you tell me where you've been the last several days?" I asked.

"What now?" Tethan cupped a hand around one earhole. The wattle of scales under her chin wobbled as she did.

I repeated myself louder. "Have you been out of the Society mansion in the past few days?"

"Oh, Great Forms no." Tethan shook her head, mouth slightly open. "My rooms, I don't leave them. They bring my dinners here. Who would feed Scampers while I was gone?"

I looked back to find the little beast following me, sniffing at my pant leg. The majus' words and the state of the apartment triggered a connection in my mind. The plate by the door probably contained some of her breakfast. If so, she would have been here eating about the time the Speaker was murdered.

"Found it!" Gompt called from the other room, and we both went to her. My colleague was holding a glistening orb nearly the size of her hairy paw. "This was stuck in the pipe. The cover was loose."

I looked at Tethan, then down at Scampers. "I think your pet may be a female," I suggested.

"Naughty Scampers!" Tethan shook a finger at the beast, who whined, then chuffed at her sandal. "Yes, yes, the egg, we will put it somewhere safe. I wondered where you went that time you got out."

Gompt gave the Tethan the egg and followed my crooked finger back to the entrance of the apartment. We left the Sathssn cooing to her pet and the thing's offspring, but before leaving her front room, I ran my finger around the topmost plate in the fallen pile by the door. I listened to the harmony between Healing and

Potential, letting the Symphony guide my sense of time. It confirmed my suspicions.

Outside, Gompt blew out a breath. "Hot enough to cook an egg in there, not just hatch one."

"At least we can mark one name off," I said.

"We may have fixed her pipes, but we're no closer," Gompt protested. "Tethan's old, but she could still have broken the geas and sent a list of names to the Speaker. You should have seen the set of chemicals and beakers in her bathroom."

I shook my head. "She said she hadn't been out of the apartment in days. All those little plates? They're the remains of old meals, sent up from the kitchen. I think Tethan is a shut-in. She could have done it, possibly, but until there's something more concrete, I think we should search elsewhere."

"I suppose she'd be terrified of the Society closing down," Gompt said. "Then there's Scampers, and Scamper's egg." She let out a sigh. "You're right. Any more names?"

I thought back. "Plithin A'Tyf. A Lobath belonging to the Houses of Communication and Healing."

"A Psychiatrist," Gompt said. "There's some definite potential to mess with how a mind's affected by the geas." We turned down another corridor.

Are there any combinations of houses that don't *have a way that might undermine the geas?*

"Isn't he the one that made the speech at the last big Society symposium where members shared their inventions?" Gompt asked. "There were more members than I've seen in one place before."

I rolled my eyes. "On the subject of 'Cooperation within the bounds of the Society'? It sounded like generic noise. Uninspired. I guess belonging to the

House of Communication doesn't guarantee good oration." We stumped down a set of stairs.

"We still need to visit him," Gompt said. "You know, just to make sure he isn't secretly plotting to overthrow the Nether."

"If he isn't, then we're back to the beginning," I said. "Speaker Thurapo isn't getting less dead, and the list of names isn't getting less lost." I looked down at my chronograph. All this traipsing around was wasting time, though I wasn't sure what else I could do. If the Society was shut down, where would I go? Technically, I had access to an apartment in the House of Potential, but everything I knew was in Poler, including what remained of the home where I grew up.

All this is assuming the two-house maji aren't put on trial once the records hidden in this mansion get out.

Majus A'Tyf was on the second level, near the front of the mansion. I straightened my coat, now some of the sweat from Tethan's apartment had dried, and we placed ourselves in front of a white door with a granite lintel.

This time Gompt knocked, and we heard a conversation cut off before someone opened the door.

Plithin A'Tyf, was short even for a Lobath, in a maroon jumpsuit, his head-tentacles wrapped up in a neat bun. He stared back with wide, surprised eyes, though that was normal for his species.

"Yes? Can I help? You two are from the workshop, aren't you? With all the new Systems? What can I do for you?" His voice was low and bubbly.

"We have a few questions—" Gompt began, but the Lobath cut him off.

"And I have answers. I remember when all the new members of the Society used to come to me. 'Unity,' I'd tell them. The Society must be a cohesive unit. Together we can go far." He stepped back. "Come on in. Meet my spouses. Always a pleasure to meet the new folk around here."

"Athera, Mieru—we have guests," he called out, and I raised a hand to stop him, but too late. Gompt and I followed, stuck in his wake.

Oh well.

Where Tethan's quarters had been warm and close, these rooms were cool and distinguished, vases on stands and artwork on the walls. Athera was taller than her husband, but a little shorter than Mieru—the wari spouse, who was of the third Lobath gender. Cups of fishy-smelling tea sat on a little table next to bowls of mushroom paste, and it was obvious we had disturbed them while they were relaxing.

"You want something to eat? We have plenty."

Refusing was futile, and we soon had our own bowls, with stiff mushroom caps to scoop out the contents. We learned neither of Plithin's spouses were maji, though they had lived in the Society for cycles.

"We accompany him to all the major functions," Mieru told us, patting hir husband's hand. I don't know what he would do without us." Athera nodded along.

Plithin laughed good naturedly. "Now what did you young ones want to ask me about? Some philosophical question about the Symphony, I suppose? That's what it usually is. You two must be about my daughter's age. She's not a majus, of course. Out at university in the Imperium. The best money can buy for our girl!"

Now Athera patted his hand. "Let them ask," she chided.

"Certainly! Ask away! Don't be afraid to come to your elders with any problems you have."

"Majus A'Tyf," I said, in a desperate attempt to stop

him before he trampled all over our words. "We have some disturbing news. I recently found evidence of a list with names of our members and Society titles, in a speaker's office. We are trying to discover how it happened."

Plithin puffed up like an angry squid. "As well you should! My spouses and I are well known to the higher societies in the Imperium, and if information about the Society got out—"

"This isn't about those volunteers you requested last month, is it?" Athera asked, and Plithin deflated.

"I don't...think so. They were all, er...compensated for the tests we ran." He turned back to us. "The geas has always been sufficient for me and my spouses to avoid any unfortunate—lapses, even when I've maybe had a few too many. That infuriating tune is quite enough to break anyone's concentration, even before it gets nasty. Surely the Society is safe?"

"Your name specifically was on a list Mandamon found," Gompt said. "And the Speaker who held it was found with his throat cut." The majus' spouses stared in horror. "We think it may be an attempt to expose the Society, and rouse public opinion against us."

"Oh." Plithin was quiet for a moment. "Oh, I see. No that would not be good at all." He stared at us with large silvery eyes. "Our friends in the Imperium know my spouses and I, yes, but not about the Society. They think we live in a nice house in Poler, not—" he trailed off, waving a long-fingered hand at their home. "You say my name was on this list? Any idea why?"

"That's what we were planning to ask you," I said. "Are you familiar with Speaker Thurapo? He was the one killed."

Mieru clapped a hand over hir mouth, stifling a gasp. Plithin looked to his mate. "Zie knows the Speaker, but only socially. I have never met him myself. How do you know my name was connected to the Society? We are all very careful with any correspondence we send, even with the geas' warning melody."

I briefly outlined the murder scene I found, and the impression of the paper I had found in the Symphony.

"Tracing it with the House of Healing—very clever," Plithin said. "I have done similar things in my time. I would love to discuss the methods you used. Did you have to change any chords, or merely listen? You hear the House of Potential too? The harmony between the houses would—" He waved Athera off. "Yes, yes, I know I am straying. I may have a moment to indulge my curiosity, even in the face of this dark news. It is the right of philosophers everywhere."

I kept my eyes firmly forward, though I desperately wanted to roll them at the Lobath's words. I had met other maji like this—who thought because they could hear the Symphony they could expound on theories of the universe better than regular people.

"We will leave you to your contemplation, majus," I began, "if you can tell us where you were yesterday night or this morning?" It was late in the afternoon by this point and I was despairing of discovering any useful information today.

The list is getting farther away.

"We were here," Athera said. "Both Mieru and I can corroborate that." The wari Lobath nodded hir head.

"And you have sent no correspondence in the last few days that could have given away this information?" I was convinced by this point, but felt I should ask.

"Certainly not." Plithin drew himself up. "If I find the miscreant who did so, I'll come to you directly. I cannot abide one who would undermine the Society and what I have with my family."

I rose, and Gompt rose with me. "Thanks for your time, majus," she said. "We'll let you know as soon as we hear anything."

"I should hope so," the majus said, leading us to the door. "The life I have built here is dear. We raised our daughter in this home. Please find whoever did this and stop them." He showed us into the hall. "Unity. It's what the Society needs, at this point more than any other. Stay safe, young ones."

Gompt and I walked down the front hallway of the mansion in silence.

"He can't have had anything to do with this," Gompt finally said. "Not with so much to lose if the Society falls."

"The daughter?" I suggested, with little conviction.

"Possible she could rebel against her parents," Gompt said, "but there's still the problem of the geas. I feel like the culprit must be a majus."

"I agree," I acknowledged with a tip of my head. "Then we are back where we started. There's no connection between the names, save ours. All six houses of the maji are represented—Strength, Communication, Power, Grace, Healing, and Potential. Who else can we go to?"

We turned into the east wing of the mansion. "Aegrino should be back," Gompt said. "Maybe he'll have more information about the Speaker."

"Good idea," I said. "He might know other members with motive, too."

"His title is 'Dancer,' yes?" Gompt asked. She wasn't as familiar with the Etanela as I was. "Strange for him to be the record keeper."

"Communication and Grace—fluid in mind and

body." I shrugged. "Helps to keep all those records in mind, I suppose."

"If he knows the names of all the members of the Society, then he's a weak point." Gompt adjusted her glasses. "There's one in every group of friends."

A valid argument, though a strange way of saying it. I knew Gompt didn't see her friend circle nearly as often as she used to. She'd complained about it while we worked with Kratitha on the System Beasts.

I brought my mind to the present. "But he couldn't possibly have given the list away. He was the one who told us about the theft."

"A good way to throw off your suspicions." Gompt tightened her bandolier of tools. "And if he is innocent, he can help us narrow down the list of members. The geas doesn't keep people from lying to us, after all." She pointed back the way we came. "Either of those maji could be spinning us a yarn, though I doubt it."

"I know." I had been thinking the same thing, but I couldn't help believing Tethan and Plithin. "Then it'll be good to ask Aegrino about the situation in the Imperium." We turned our steps toward the record room, passing other maji deep in conversation.

Now everyone looks suspicious. Why are those two whispering? Who would want to do the Society ill?

In short order we reached the records room, near the center of the mansion and Moortlin's office. I would have updated the Benish on what we'd found, but they had gone back to the Spire of the Maji in the Imperium. They were busy, being on the Council.

The record room seemed empty, and I wondered if Aegrino was still in the Imperium, too. It should be easy to spot the tall Etanela.

"He made a portal back in the shelves when we left,"

I said, turning a corner into a tight path between book-
cases. They were higher than my head, stuffed with
books, rolled papers, ideas, contraptions, and other, less
identifiable objects.

I stopped short. Aegrino Plumera Lunigi was lying
face down on the floor, a puddle of greenish blood
pooling beneath his chest.

PART THREE

More Than One

- *When I applied to be the record keeper for the Society, little did I realize the extent of the accounts Moortlin collected over the cycles. I have piles of notes on wartime uses of the Symphony rendered illegal by the Council, forgotten inventions, and secrets that could tip the politics of the Great Assembly to the benefit of a single species. It is little wonder our leader is paranoid about others finding us out. The Society may have more dangerous information stored than the rest of the maji combined.*

Aegrino Plumera Lunigi, Record Keeper for the Society of Two Houses

"Gompt!" I called. My friend came running, then skidded to a halt, bracing herself against a bookshelf to keep from stepping in the puddle of blood.

"Oh no! Is he...?"

I knelt by the body, pressing a hand to the back of his neck. Still warm, but there was no rise and fall of breath, no movement.

"It must have been recently. It's only been a few lightenings since Moortlin and I spoke with him. If he cleaned up the Speaker's study, he can't have been back for long either. Help me turn him."

Gompt came forward, one paw over her mouth, but hesitated. "Shouldn't we go to someone—?" She looked around as if one of the Poler Civic Watch would materialize out of the woodwork.

"Who are we going to tell?" I asked, sitting back on my heels. "We are in a mansion filled with suspects, in an organization with a geas keeping it secret. We can't let anyone outside know, and we can't trust anyone on the inside. Now come help."

Gompt grimaced, but reluctantly came forward. She was obviously uncomfortable, but together, we lifted Aegrino's corpse, bluish arms flopping lifelessly.

The body had not stiffened yet, and our actions revealed the method of the record keeper's death. There were vicious slashes across the front of the Etanela's robe, parting both fabric and flesh. Gompt hissed and covered her mouth again, and I barely kept from jumping to my feet. The cuts were to the bone, vitriol and blood dripping from fierce lines of violence.

"What could cut a body like that?" she asked. "It's like the killer was in a rage."

"But there's no sign of a struggle," I said. "At least not from what I can see. Just like Speaker Thurapo." I forced myself to stay over the body, though my mind screamed at me of what happened this morning, and two cycles ago.

"What about the Symphony of Healing?" Gompt said, and I nodded, already listening for the strains of music. *Losing myself in the music is always calming.*

The melody of Healing around Aegrino's body was ragged, almost doubled, arpeggios cutting off and resuming in a different key like two pieces were playing at once. The usual forte measures of exertion were not present.

"He didn't fight, or even move much before getting gutted," I said. "What could have done this with such speed?"

"Maybe the Symphony of Potential can tell us." Gompt's eyes were far away again behind her glasses, and I could tell she was listening to our shared house. I transitioned from the music of Healing to Potential, like changing from a wind quartet to a drum solo.

The melody of Potential was a different thing from Healing, from warm to cold, organic to artificial. Potential was the song of logic and forces.

"There," Gompt said. "That repeating cadenza, with the descending fourths." I waded through the music, searching for the same part of the arrangement. It was situated around the wounds, like the broken measures in the Symphony of Healing.

"What does it mean?" I asked. Gompt was better than I at deriving history from Potential alone.

She mimed a path at head level through the air, in time with the beat of the music. It would have been at chest level for the Etanela. The same place his wounds were centered.

"It's like he was slashed by a bunch of blades, all at once," Gompt said, screwing her snout up so her canines showed. "I keep our metal and woodworking tools that sharp, and there are other rooms in the mansion where corpses are dissected. The implement could have come from any of them. It's ghastly."

I opened myself to both Symphonies, the organic rhythms of Healing meshing with the syncopation of Potential. I blinked in surprise as I realized the disruptions in one piece of music matched the spirited sections of the other. The Symphony of Potential had literally cleaved the Symphony of Healing in twain.

"Interesting. This is not a normal injury." *I just can't understand why.* I pushed my glasses up. Something was nagging at me, begging for connection with some fact I knew intimately, but it made no sense. "This must have been done by someone Aegrino knew."

"Did Aegrino let the killer come to the mansion through a portal? Did he even finish cleaning up Speaker Thurapo's body?" Gompt put her paws on her furry hips and looked away from the mess. "It makes no sense. There's no way Aegrino invited the killer here, but they were able to get from the Imperium to Poler just as quickly as him. I'd bet Nether glass it's a Society majus. It's got to be."

"But why?" I stroked my beard. "There's little reason for one of the Society to betray their own. Here we have safety, freedom to research and escape from persecution, others who think as we do—what's the motive?"

"Too much ambition? Jealousy? Just not satisfied with something?" Gompt shrugged. "Could be anything. Finding the perpetrator is the quickest way to the motive."

I wasn't convinced. If we knew the *why,* that would lead us to the *who* and the *how.* There had to be a solid reason a second person—a second Etanela—was killed on the same day. I moved back from Aegrino's body, feeling like I should do something with him. *If we can find another clue here, it may lead us to the killer.*

"What about his records?" I asked. Gompt looked around as if they would appear out of the air. "What if he had another copy of the Society names? Could the killer have lost the first copy somehow?"

"Let's look around." I was grasping at ideas, distracted and half expecting officials to come knocking at the mansion door. Whoever had the list could have gone to anyone in the Assembly, especially since this person knew where the mansion was and how to get past the complex System installed at the front gate. Normally, it caused others to overlook the mansion, in a similar manner to how the geas kept us from speaking of the Society. Maybe it wasn't working anymore.

We looked around the records room, led by dips and trills in the Symphony of Potential to follow Aegrino's path. It was almost random, as if the majus was not familiar with his library.

Gompt called out, "Aha!" a few minutes later. I ran to where she was bent over in front of a small cabinet, stuffed with records so ancient they were more dust than text. She had a roll of parchment in her hand with recent writing at the end of a long list of names.

I took the sheet gingerly, tuning a few chords of the music of Potential to a lower key to prevent my fingers from causing any more destruction to the ancient list. I read from the bottom up, noting names of some older members I recognized, leading back in time. Tethan and Plithin were both on there. I rolled the scroll backwards, noting Moortlin's name about a third of the way up. There were cycles noted for many of the names, with substantial gaps in places. The oldest reached into the single digits.

"Gompt," I breathed, "The oldest of these names are almost a thousand cycles old. They reach all the way back to the Aridori war."

Gompt shivered. "I don't need any more nightmares. Growing up, my friend group would tell us tales of Aridori, sneaking about and making off with naughty children, taking their place and causing chaos. Stick to the present."

I rolled the scroll to the end. Neither I nor my two friends were on the list. It was an older copy, but likely one Aegrino had used to make a new version. Indeed, the Symphony of Potential had a soft chorus drifting into silence: the action of copying information from this place to another, but the music was too faint to determine where the new list was located.

"This is useless," I said. "It's not complete, and the new sheet is missing. Even if we found it, we're back to sifting through however many members of the Society there are at the moment."

I sagged back against a bookcase. I couldn't do this. If the Society was shut down, I had no place to go. My family was gone, and our old house had been sold last cycle. I put the scroll on a nearby shelf and held my head in my hands.

Gompt was there in an instant. "What's the problem?" she asked. "What can I do?"

I shook my head. "It's nothing."

"It's not nothing," Gompt told me. "The Society can't be shut down so easily. The Council has to know something about us. I can't believe Moortlin—and over a hundred maji—have kept this place a complete secret, even with the geas. Some shred of evidence must have gotten out before now."

I looked up at my friend. "But where would we all go, if the mansion was closed? Think about Plithin and his family. About Tethan and Scampers." *That's not the only reason.*

I hadn't told Gompt about the accident with my family. Moortlin was the only one who knew.

"Every majus has an apartment in the Imperium," Gompt said. "If the Society closed, we could live there."

"I've never lived in the Imperium," I said. It came out almost by accident and I closed my mouth. Gompt looked at me strangely.

"How—" her brow drew down behind her glasses. "What about classes in the Imperium? Living with your mentor while apprenticed?"

"I...we commuted," I said.

"That would take a lot of money, even for a majus," Gompt said. "Using a portal to arrive in the Imperium every day? Leaving at night for home? Did you come from Methiem?"

I was already sweeping my hands side to side, negating her words. *It's not like that. Not anything like that.* A memory intruded—my mother watching while my future mentor stood beside me, the rusty brown of the House of Potential visible to us both. Abarham was leading me through my first attempt at changing notes in the Symphony of Potential. We were in my house, after a lunch with my parents' good friend and his husband.

Abarham Garhuk. The thought of my old mentor—practically another father—made a lump rise in my throat, and my hand rise to my scar. The emotion was stronger than my reaction to either the Speaker's or the record keeper's death, and I was still in the same room as the latter's corpse. Poler was a large, but quiet town, and an insular community; relationships were long-lasting. When my mother's childhood friend discovered we could hear the same aspect of the Great Symphony, a bond formed between us instantly. There was no doubt I would apprentice with him.

"I grew up in Poler," I said. "Right here in this town. My family—" My hesitation only lasted a heartbeat. I pushed away the feelings climbing up my chest. "My family knew the person who later became my mentor—Majus Garhuk."

I waited for the realization to catch up to Gompt. It always took a few seconds, when people heard his name.

She blinked furiously behind her glasses. "Wait...you mean Majus Garhuk, who was killed in Poler two cycles ago?"

I nodded. "The same. Most people pay attention to the high profile name in that story, but not much else." *Not to the other names.*

"What do you mean—" Gompt broke off, looking to the ceiling of the records room. This was not the first time I had been seated only a few paces from a rapidly cooling corpse.

My Festuour friend looked back, concern on her ursine face. "A local family was with the majus when he died, in a strange disturbance. No one could ever figure out how one room had collapsed when the rooms next to it were whole. That was—that was your family?"

I knew the look on my face was confirmation enough.

"Oh, Mandamon, I'm sorrier than you can imagine," Gompt said. She reached out, putting a paw on my shoulder, and squeezed. I placed my hand on her paw, feeling the fine fur on her three wide-spread digits.

"I've only been out of the Nether twice," I admitted, "both times to my grandparent's villa on Methiem, in Ibra." I took in a deep breath, breaking the bubble of memory that surrounded us.

I can't break down now.

"But that's in the past. If the Society is shut down, I suppose I'll get an apartment in the Imperium, and find out what the big city is really like." I made an effort to stop my mouth from turning down.

"Hey, you're welcome to stay with me!" Gompt said. "My friend group has a set of apartments in Mid Imperium, and there's always room for one more." Her furry brow creased. "At least there was the last time I was there."

"Maybe I will," I said, and wiped at my eyes behind my glasses. "Though the first thing is to prevent anything happening to the Society." *Friend group. Always one more.* The thought brought something that had been lurking in my subconscious to the fore.

"Wait—we listened to the music around Aegrino's

death," I said, and Gompt nodded. "So why didn't we hear the notes of whoever *killed* him?"

Gompt stood up straight as I pushed away from the bookcase. "You're right. I should have heard some music around those knives that killed him. Who wielded them, and how? Rot and claw, I can't believe you trust me to help you designing complex Systems for these automatons." She fished the little Festuour System Beast out of her bandolier.

I contemplated Gompt's little figurine as we approached Aegrino's corpse. "I missed it too. That's why we're working together."

Gompt saw where I was looking and held it up. "Mechanical," she said. "Sort of like the music, isn't it?"

"Just what I was thinking," I said. I listened to the System behind the little model. The beat, the key, even the tempo was like the faint echoes of the slashes on Aegrino's body. Systems did not occur in nature, but were created by maji. They never had the same beauty as naturally arising music—the Grand Symphony.

"This was done with a System," I said. "The murderer has a weapon made by a majus, or stolen from one." There was some part of this that still felt too familiar, but I couldn't place it.

Gompt cocked her head from side to side, tapping her fingers to some beat I couldn't hear. It must be the House of Grace.

"Aegrino was a Dancer—Communication and Grace. Someone who could change the Symphony of Grace could waltz right out of the reach of whatever slashed him." She waved her paw holding the figurine at the corpse, keeping it out of her sightline. Her other hand was tapping at the air, as if touching points on an intricate diagram. "There's no residue in the music. None of the scales are interrupted and all the chords are in place. If Aegrino had used the Symphony to move out of the way, I would still be able to hear it."

"Maybe another aspect can tell us more." I braced myself, and bent over the body. The Symphony of Healing was a faint whisper. The body's mechanisms were breaking down, even in the few minutes we had been here. I stood. There should be music here describing another person, but all the phrases seemed to define Aegrino's body, ragged and fragmented as they were. Gompt's and my measures were forte and in the foreground. It was unnatural. There was something we were both missing.

"If I had some part of the weapon the attacker used," I mused, "I could trace who held it with Potential and Healing combined." *Just like when I traced the paper the Speaker held.*

"What about the...the wounds?" Gompt suggested. "There may be a piece stuck...inside." She looked away, and I think if Festuour had less fur, I'd have seen her turning green.

"Good idea." Physical contact was helpful for both my Symphonies. I took in a deep breath, then ran a finger down the tattered strip along Aegrino's chest. As I touched the jagged flesh, several themes popped to the forefront, first a spiraling chord progression in the house of Healing—the identifier every being held within them. The music bled to everything a person touched, and was unique.

Second was a martial beat in the music of Potential, decaying from a high register to a lower one. As seconds passed, the rhythm evolved in a regular manner. Try as I might, I could only hear one spiraling chord, with some minor variations, though that could have been an artifact of Etanela biology. There was only Aegrino here. Had he somehow killed himself?

I wiped my fingers on a clean section of Aegrino's coat, used a few notes in the Symphony of Healing to burn away any other contamination, then straightened.

"There is nothing else." I let my face show my puzzlement. "Maybe Moortlin will have another idea. We have to tell them what happened, anyway."

Gompt agreed, and we made our way out of the record room and down the hall, leaving Aegrino's body behind. Hopefully Moortlin would have a way to clean it up. It wasn't like there had never been death in the mansion.

It was late in the afternoon, and the head of the Society spent their evenings in the mansion. We knocked on Moortlin's door, but even with repeated knocking and calling out, there was no answer.

We were about to leave, and bring Kratitha up to date on our findings instead, when a small noise caught my ear—the liquid *pop* of a portal opening.

I held one finger up to Gompt and knocked again.

This time there was rhythmic stumping, and Moortlin's burnished face peered out at us from the opened door.

"Yes? These ones have caught one, hm, between meetings. One has little time for—"

"Aegrino is dead," I cut Moortlin off. Their solid yellow eyes flashed bright for a second, and they pulled the door open.

"Come in then, and, hm, tell one what has occurred."

We quickly told the Benish about Tethan and Plithin, and how we found Aegrino, plus the lack of information on the killer.

"It has to be a majus in the Society," I finished, "but

they have hidden their tracks too well. Neither Gompt nor I know what else to do. And, someone will need to deal with Aegrino and the mess in the records room."

Moortlin paced to a chorus of creaks. "One cannot accept anyone inside the Society would do such a thing. One has, hm, personally interviewed every two-house majus over the last several hundred cycles. Care was taken to avoid any personalities with attributes leading to a situation such as this. This is very disturbing."

"If it wasn't someone in the Society, then who was it?" Gompt asked. "If someone got in here, easy as you please, that means this place isn't as secret as you make it out. Is the geas not working? Is the System at the gates broken? You can't have it both ways."

"This one is correct that there is more happening than on, hm, first inspection." Moortlin's eyes dimmed. "Was there anything to suggest another avenue of investigation? Both victims were Etanela. Is this a, hm, specist crime?

We all looked at each other, but I shook my head. "It doesn't...feel like it," I said. "Why go to all this trouble to invade the Society? There are other Etanela members who haven't been harmed, and the Speaker wasn't a majus."

"If it was about Etanela, then why that method of murder? Why steal the list?" Gompt asked.

"Perhaps one could accompany these ones back. With four of the six houses accounted for, surely these ones must discover—"

Moortlin broke off as Gompt jumped, clapping a hand to her belt. "What in blazes?" she cried, fumbling with the buckle. "The friendless thing is trying to stab me!"

"What is?" I asked, as Gompt drew the System Beast model from her pouch. The little hands were waving in all directions, tiny fingers stabbing in the air. The Symphony of Potential around it was spiky with glissandos and trills. Gompt almost dropped it as one little hand gouged her finger.

"Ow! Little thing is haywire!" She juggled it from one paw to the other, trying to keep it from stabbing her.

"If this is how these System Beasts function, one does not have high hopes for the proposal," Moortlin said, stepping away.

"It's never done that before," I said. "What could possibly make a System Beast act like this?"

That was when the screaming started.

PART FOUR

System Beast

- System Beasts will form a new type of service to the members of the Great Assembly of Species. They can be geared in a number of roles, from laborer or draftbeast, to social secretary or aide for those with disabilities, or even items of luxury. The possibilities are nearly limitless, as the constructs can be quite intelligent and take orders well. I look forward to seeing how the people of the Nether receive and apply System Beasts to make their lives easier.

From a proposal by Mandamon Feldo, majus of the Houses of Healing and Potential

The three of us rushed into the hallway to find lights blinking, and rumbles echoing through the walls of the mansion. A majus ran past, carrying a bucket of water.

"The kitchen is on fire!" she yelled over her shoulder.

It wasn't just Gompt's System Beast that was malfunctioning. All of the Systems in the mansion had gone crazy. In this place full of maji, I hardly thought about how many Systems were hidden in the walls to drive water uphill, heat rooms, and even light corridors when the walls of the Nether had dimmed for the night.

Moortlin stumped away down the hall in the opposite direction from the running majus. "One will recruit all maji who can hear the Symphony of Potential," they called in a voice like splitting wood. "Those are the only ones who can deactivate the Systems."

"We'll help anyone we can," I called back, but then Gompt took my arm, and I turned to her.

"Kratitha," she said. The fur on her shoulders was standing on end.

My eyes widened, and I ran after my colleague. The Pixie was surrounded by the most advanced Systems ever made in the Nether, and couldn't hear the House of Potential. The System Beasts would tear her apart!

Our workshop was down several flights of stairs and in a different wing of the mansion. While we ran, scenes of chaos intruded on us—burst pipes spewing water from walls, broken and sparking lanterns, and several rooms filled with the roar of flames. But maji were everywhere, battling the mayhem. All six colors of the Symphony glowed around walls, ceiling, and Society members like a mad kaleidoscope.

I listened to the Symphonies of Healing and Potential as I ran, but the music was dissonant, with too many changes happening at once. I could do little to help those who already fought the chaos, even if I wanted to. The Systems weren't only turning off or malfunctioning. It was as if their notes were being released in the most chaotic manner possible.

Finally we arrived at the workshop, and Gompt worried at the doorknob before thrusting it open and rushing in.

It looked as if a hundred people cluttered the room rather than just one, and all were clambering to get to the little Pixie in their midst. Light glinted from moving limbs, and my eye was drawn around the workshop, colors flickering in and out of existence as different Systems moved our constructs around.

In the middle danced the Ethulina pullbeast we intended to show to the Great Assembly, striking out with its front hooves and snorting clouds of steam, though Kratitha wove and danced away from it, avoiding a confrontation. Every bit of damage we did taking it down meant that much more work in repairs. We'd be destroying our own days of labor.

Kratitha was a blur of motion, her wings keeping her just above the floor and away from the smallest, reaching System Beasts. Her body glowed blue with the House of Grace and bright orange with the House of Power. She coordinated every move perfectly, and the Pixie hummed along with the music she heard, so deep in concentration was she. Her complicated voice box picked off paired chords and harmonics, and despite myself I paused a moment to listen.

I think that's the closest I've ever come to hearing the Symphony of Grace.

Gompt also flowed into the Symphony of Grace, insinuating her thick body between two strutting peacock-shaped Beasts who lashed out with filed metal talons. Neither touched a hair of her pelt.

Kratitha was the only one of our trio who couldn't change the Symphony of Potential in order to shut down the Systems. Instead, a spear of orange accompanied her tiny hand, showing she was adjusting the Symphony of Power. She inserted her hand between the head and body of a bulky dog-like automaton, twisting at just the right angle, then jerked and the head popped to one side. The clanking Beast listed and plowed into a wall. Not a big loss, as that design was meant to test the walking mechanisms.

A metal claw struck the doorframe a handbreadth from my ear and I jolted back. The malfunctioning System Beasts were angling toward me and, I belatedly realized, toward Gompt. They weren't just attacking Kratitha, but any person within range.

Or any majus?

I fell into the music of Potential, hearing an overlapping stream of clanking, whistles, and shrieks. The music associated with Systems was artificial, lacking the beauty of the natural music of the universe. That meant it was easier to disrupt. I laid a hand on the head of a crawling lizard System Beast that came to my knee, keeping away from the wooden hinged jaw full of teeth.

Why did we ever put teeth in these things?

The foundational beat held the Beast's mechanisms together—the cognitive gearing tied to the movement actuators tied to the structural frequencies. I dropped the beat to a lower register and the lizard Beast jerked to a halt. One down, and—how many to go? We'd made over a hundred of the things in the past five months.

Gompt reached Kratitha and powered down one of the larger prototypes as I had. Its mouth sagged open instead of sinking into the Pixie's flesh.

I moved forward, avoiding clumsy thrusts, slashes and even attempts by two or three System Beasts to gang up on me, disconnecting the Systems as I did. Some part of my brain rejoiced, realizing our creations were working in concert, though we had not yet programmed that level of sophistication.

The Ethulina seemed almost to be coordinating the assault. Every time it tossed its head toward us, or kicked out a leg to strike, smaller System Beasts would swarm in around it.

The three of us moved together, each familiar with the others and overlapping in aspects of the Grand Symphony. Gompt and I shut down Systems, leaving a trail of System Beasts in mid-stride, or crawl. Kratitha moved with a butterfly-like grace, flitting between smaller opponents and the pullbeast, taunting it away from attacking while making thrusts augmented by the Symphony of Power. She left orange auras washing over the other colors of the Systems, disrupting how they interacted. She did the least damage she could to each construct, while leaving it incapable of further function.

I quickened notes in the Symphony of Healing, toning muscles in my legs. They would ache later, but doing so allowed me to keep up with Gompt, who flowed—a furry dancer—through the thick of our creations, stopping each one with a deft touch.

It took minutes, or a whole lightening, I wasn't sure which. But finally, only the Ethulina prototype—the ringleader—still moved. None of us wished to damage it, or disrupt the fine-tuned System keeping it running. We'd been circling it, deactivating the simpler System Beasts first.

We'd created the Ethulina pullbeast with fantastical materials instead of the flesh and feathers of the native Kirian fauna, but it pranced and cavorted like a real creature. It shook its crystal mane with a chime of glass as its haunches—reflective metal above ranks of wooden scales—bunched and caught the overhead light. Gompt and I flanked it carefully while Kratitha buzzed in the background, calling out unhelpful admonitions not to injure the thing.

I dodged a flailing front hoof, its joints expanded into a dexterous hand, while Gompt stepped in from the back. She tried to lay a paw on the automaton long enough to sort through iterations of music formed from our notes and the Symphony of Potential.

"You'll have to use both houses," I called to my friend, and I fell deeper into both the House of Potential and Healing. Keeping both Symphonies present in my consciousness was like swimming against two currents, each trying to drag me down.

I doubled the chords of melody in my skin, then tripled them, taking notes from the core of my being and making my skin temporarily much thicker, covered in a sheen of white from the House of Healing. Gompt used the House of Grace to dodge the System Beast's quick slashes, as evidenced by the aura of blue surrounding her.

An iron hand-hoof grazed my arm, impacting my hardened skin. More bruises later to go with aching muscles, but at least the strike hadn't broken anything.

Finally, Gompt grasped a forelimb firmly enough to keep it from another strike, and I moved in close, both hands on its metal and wood flanks. I flinched as a back leg kicked at my shins, but held my contact against its side.

The Symphony of Potential was a riot, with what should have been an arrangement of ordered solos and duets corrupted and tangled together. It would take time to sort, and would cost Gompt and I more notes from our beings. Without damaging the System more, I searched for the connecting node in the midst of it, buried between five louder pieces of music clamoring for my attention.

I grasped the notes that connected that System to the others and yanked them free. They had originated from my music in the first place, and the notes settled back in my core like old socks stretched past their original use. The creature stuttered and came to a halt.

The workshop fell quiet, save for the rustling of wooden limbs against wire mesh. A System Beast in the shape of a turtle clamored against its cage, still making its bid for freedom.

I let out a long breath and turned to the others.

"Will have to rebalance all servos before taking it to Assembly," Kratitha said. She dabbed at several cuts on her arms, which dripped a brownish blood.

I took back the notes I had added to the melody of my skin, rejoining them to the core of my being, like cool water poured on a burn. I rotated one forearm, watching a blotch of green and purple that was forming. *That will hurt later.*

"I think that's the least of our problems," I said. "This was obviously some sort of attack or distraction related to the two murders."

"Two murders?" Kratitha looked up from tending her wounds.

"Aegrino is dead, too," Gompt said. She looked unharmed, but there were several places where her fur was matted and mussed, and she held one paw to her side. "Someone is trying their hardest to make sure the Society crumbles in on itself, both emotionally and physically," she gestured to the ceiling by the doorframe, where a steady drip of water was beginning in one corner.

"Then what do we do?" I asked. "We have very little to go on, no suspects, and whoever is doing this seems to have more control over our Systems than we do." I paused, frowning. There was still something nagging me about that.

"Help Moortlin?" Kratitha suggested.

"We should see how many others of the House of Potential they found to help," Gompt said. "We can assist in shutting down other Systems in the mansion if they haven't finished."

I shrugged a shoulder in acceptance of her point, but it felt like giving in, somehow. *The head of the Society is counting on* me *to figure out what happened.*

"Yes. I have cleaning to do here, and servo recalibration," Kratitha agreed, shooing us with one hand. Then she twitched, mouth tightening, and placed her fingers over a particularly wide and shallow cut on the other forearm.

"Will you be all right here?" I was not very good at regenerating flesh with the Symphony of Healing—it was a rare talent—but Kratitha waved me away.

"Others with worse. Tend to them. Find out who did this. I will set things right in workshop."

I looked to Gompt, who shrugged. "Let's go find Moortlin, then," she said.

On the way there, Gompt helped tie a sling on an older Methiemum while I listened to the trills of pain running through his music. I turned a few from sixteenth to eighth notes, dimming the worst. He thanked us both, then went back to his job of keeping water flowing through this section of the mansion, despite a large crack in one pipe. The blue of the House of Grace and the green of The House of Strength surrounded him.

Near the stairs to the next level, we helped a Sureri woman with an elegant coif of hair. Auras of green and yellow—the Houses of Strength and Communication— kept the ceiling from totally collapsing, though a portion had already fallen in. Two Sureriaj males—her partners, I supposed—were picking pieces of plaster off her. I knew her by name, though the species was stingy with sharing that information.

I listened to the Symphony of Healing. "Majus Zuege, I don't hear any bones broken, though you'll have bruises more impressive than my own. Is there anything else we can do?"

"Well, I thank yer, but no," she said gravely. "Go off an' bodge together some aught folks with ills. There's plenty injured more than meself."

We found Moortlin on the highest floor of the mansion, brushing wood and plaster dust from their rough hide. Much of the shedding skin that told of their age had been scraped away. We confirmed they had found others in the House of Potential, and deactivated most of the other Systems.

"The damage is, hm, extensive," they said, "though the worst is under control. The time to repair the mansion will be, hm, lengthy. One has not seen such chaos in one's time as the head of the Society." They let out a great gust of breath, like wind through branches, and slapped more dust from their skin.

"There is something more going on here, obviously," I said. I hoped Moortlin would have some other information for us, despite the chaos.

"There is," they agreed, and their unblinking yellow eyes stared between Gompt and I. "Before recent events, one was going to suggest this group, hm, attend to Aegrino's body. Now is not the best time, but this one believes it is necessary to learn more."

I traded a glance with Gompt, not sure what more we could learn from that source, though we could at least give him some dignity. *Poor Aegrino. No one deserves that fate, and he was a good record keeper.*

When we got back to the records room, Moortlin stumping along behind us, we were confronted with an empty patch of hardwood floor. Aegrino's body was gone.

I spun to the others. "Where did he go?" Gompt's eyes were wide behind her glasses and even Moortlin stood stock still, dazed.

"These ones are, hm, *certain* Aegrino is dead?" Moortlin ventured.

"I'm certain." I said, as Gompt said, "He's definitely dead."

"We listened to the Symphony around his body," I added. "I've seen death before. The melodies were breaking down in the same way."

"Then who did this?" Gompt asked. She paced around the spot where the Etanela's body had been until a short time ago, peering at the jointed oak floor. "Were the haywire Systems just a distraction?" The pool of blood was gone as well, and the space had been cleaned and tidied, as if nothing had happened, despite water dripping from a burst pipe overhead.

My Festuour friend bent until her snout almost touched the wood planks. "There's still a stain here, but it's faint. Whoever cleaned was faster than a racing thrint in heat."

"The confusion would have covered much," Moortlin rumbled, and I checked my chronograph.

Another lightening-and-a-half gone dealing with haywire Systems.

"Still, what one would have the, hm, ability to do such a thing?" My mentor took their own turn around the place where the record keeper died. "To affect so many Systems at once, and to do things they had not originally been composed to do—it is as if one majus has been multiplied into several." They turned back. "This reminds one of the work this one conducted on harmonic resonances, Mandamon."

I froze, my palms tingling, then sweating. *That's what has been nagging at me.* It acted similar to one of my first inventions—the most dangerous. Similar in method, yes, but there was no way it could have affected an area this size. Plus, I had torn the thing apart!

It was also what caused Moortlin to invite me to the Society, despite the accident. Despite me losing all I held dear.

I leaned against a bookshelf. It was *not* the same. 'Harmonic resonances' was just a fancy way of saying different actions were amplified by each other. I had the idea to link Systems people used into one big mechanism. Imagine being able to control heat, water, and power sources in one System. People could even have carried the resonator around with them, turning Systems off and on with a simple switch.

However, mingling so many Systems proved unstable. Every time I used my invention, at least one of them failed. I thought I could fix it. I thought I could accommodate the fluctuations in the Grand Symphony all by myself.

Right up until the day Abarham and my family died.

I'd recycled some of the safer ideas into the concept of the System Beast, but I'd never touched the harmonic resonator again. I'd purposefully tried to forget it, after dismantling the device.

"The resonator can't have caused this." My voice was weak, barely more than a whisper. I forced my hand away from fingering the groove below my right eye. "No one else knows how to use it, and it could never affect the whole mansion, unless modified greatly."

"One is not suggesting anything," Moortlin said. "One knows this is a, hm, delicate subject. Merely that the mechanism is, hm, comparable." My mentor was contrite, their eyes dim. "One is confident this one did not cause this disruption. All invited to the Society are personally interviewed, and one holds them in highest regard. That includes Mandamon Feldo."

"It had to be someone inside," Gompt insisted. She was watching me, warily. "But Mandamon has been with me. I don't think he took the list of members, and he certainly couldn't have moved Aegrino's body."

"It wasn't me," I said, my voice a little stronger. "But I may have enabled whoever did this." Gompt stepped back, but my mind was not on her.

Where did I leave the pieces? When was the last time I saw it? I could not bring myself to completely destroy it, no matter what it had caused.

"Then these ones must continue to investigate," Moortlin said. "One must direct the maji in cleaning and repair of the mansion, and move those whose apartments have been affected." They sighed again and unfolded thick fingers toward Gompt and I. "Please inform one the moment these ones find anything."

With that, the Benish stumped from the room, leaving me to stare at the spot on the floor where a dead body no longer lay. Gompt was watching me.

Finally, I stared back. "It wasn't me," I repeated.

She nodded. "I believe you. But Mandamon, you've had something that could cause this much destruction, just lying around?"

"No. It couldn't have done this." I shook my head. "This would have required heavy modifications, by someone who knew what they were doing. It was supposed to help people." My words were helpless.

"Come on then," Gompt said. "Let's see if your gadget is still there before you work yourself even deeper into a funk. Maybe you're keying yourself up for nothing."

We walked in silence to my room, on a lower floor, not far from the workshop. Broken wood, pipes, and people surrounded us. A plank from the ceiling had fallen in front of my door and my hand shook as I reached for it.

So similar to the destruction in the accident, but on such a greater scale.

Inside, I stared around, digging into the memories of where I'd left the resonator. I went to a cabinet on one wall, jerking open the doors and reaching for a lower drawer, kept closed since I had arrived in the mansion. There was dust inside the drawer, outlining two long shapes where there should have been pieces of my invention.

I sank to the floor.

PART FIVE

Homebrew

- What is the relation between a majus and their family? Would-be maji are often recognized early in life, as I was, and encouraged to live at their House in the Imperium. For maji who are still very young, the Council allows guardians to live with them. However, there is always a drive to separate the one who can hear the Symphony from those who can't. This is counterintuitive, as maji are also encouraged to marry and have families. If a family or friend group such as mine becomes too large for the small apartments in the Houses of the Maji, that group is given a stipend from the Council to find a place to live nearby. This setup both insulates maji from the rest of the Great Assembly of Species, and incorporates them as progenitor of new family lines, setting the status of "majus" higher than other beings.

Part of an essay on the social impact of the maji, by Timpomitnob Gompt, Watcher, of the Houses of Grace and Potential

Gompt stood over me, paws on her hips, below her bandolier of tools. "It wasn't you, Mandamon," she said. "You didn't do this. I don't think you killed the Speaker, and I know you didn't kill Aegrino. Someone stole your invention, and they made it do these horrible things. It must be someone inside the Society, whatever Moortlin says."

I shook my head. *Could I have fixed the resonator and then blocked it out?* I didn't remember my studies for the ten-day after the accident. But that was two cycles ago, and it hadn't happened again. *At least I don't think so.*

"Even if it wasn't me, this couldn't have happened *without* me," I told my friend. "I am responsible, in some manner. Just like I was responsible when my parents and Abarham—" I cut off, my throat refusing to speak the words. Gompt was silent, and I thought she would agree with me. I looked up.

Her face was scrunched, almost into a growl, her brows pulled low behind her glasses. I don't know if she'd even heard me. "What is it?" I said, fearing her words would only be a condemnation.

"Which person is liable to tinker with inventions that aren't their own, make things work in a new manner, or neglect to tell others about their changes?"

I didn't even have to think. "Those are all things Kratitha does if...oh." I rubbed my suddenly cold hands together. It made a sick kind of sense.

The three of us had all been in each other's rooms. We shared thoughts and designs constantly. I'm sure I'd mentioned my research on harmonic resonance at some point. *Did I ever mention the controller wand?* I looked to the empty drawer, where the lines free of dust sat like an accusation.

I kept most of my work in the shop with the others. Aside from the cabinet, a writing desk with one stack of paper, my bed, and my closet, my room was empty. It would be easy to find something hidden, especially for an inquisitive Pixie good at getting into where she didn't belong.

"Back to the workshop," I said, and Gompt gave a sharp nod. It still didn't make any sense. *Why would Kratitha modify my resonator, then set it on herself?* I couldn't believe the Pixie could kill someone, and she abhorred destruction like the resonator caused.

A few minutes later we were back in the chaos of our workshop, broken System Beasts lying as if they had fainted. Kratitha was not there.

"Again? What is going on?" Gompt paced ahead, auras of brown and blue surrounding her. I was not sure what she was looking for in the Symphonies of Grace and Potential. From what I gathered about the combination we called an Archeologist, the House of Grace augmented patterns in music, revealing objects out of place or sequence in the House of Potential's notes.

"Here," Gompt said, pointing to a small patch on the floor. She was near the inert Ethulina pullbeast, one hoof still raised. "I think this is Kratitha's blood."

I moved closer. "She was bleeding from fighting against the System Beasts."

"This is different." Gompt walked a few paces away. "Those drops start here, and spiral out as she fought." Her furry fingers traced a spiral of brown droplets spread around the room, flung like a dance partner spinning around their mate. Now Gompt pointed them out, it was a beautiful pattern, in a way. I traced arcs and swirls with my hand, imagining the Pixie slipping impossibly between attackers, while delivering perfectly timed strikes.

"But here," Gompt drew my attention to the original spot, "this breaks the pattern, and there's only one spot. It happened after everything else, probably after you and I left."

I let the Symphonies of Healing and Potential fill me, listening to notes curling around the brown stain. The measures were changing key, organic compounds oxidizing. The notes defining the energy quieted as the blood cooled, and there was a definite difference between this spot and others around the room.

"I agree," I said, frowning. "This blood was shed after the rest. She exerted herself and made her wounds bleed again."

"Or something was done *to* her?" Gompt suggested.

"First you say Kratitha took my device, now someone else is responsible?" I crossed my arms. From the moment I saw Speaker Thurapo's corpse this morning, nothing made sense. Had Aegrino cleaned the scene before he was killed in turn, or were Imperium guard on their way, even now? There was something missing.

"I can't believe she did all this, Mandamon," Gompt said. She played with the frame of her glasses where Kratitha had fixed it. "She was fighting the System Beasts when we got here. Why would she have caused this chaos only to be attacked?"

"Maybe she didn't think it through. This is Kratitha we're talking about." But my words had no weight behind them.

"Think what through?" Gompt asked. "Bringing down the mansion and the Society? Why would she do that? Her caste is dying off, Mandamon—you know that. This is the last place she has."

Just like me. I knew the Pixie was at odds with her people, but Gompt was closer to her than I was. I hadn't known she was in exile.

"So let's find her," I said. "Maybe she went to her room."

But Kratitha was not in her room, or in the medical facilities, or anywhere else in the mansion we could determine. Gompt and I met back in the workshop half a lightening later.

"Was there anyone else in here?" We searched the workshop, with our eyes and the Symphonies, but the music of her passage was fading, and Kratitha seemed to have been the only one present.

"She is of the House of Power," I said. "Good at showing connections between places and things. Perhaps she realized something about the murders."

Gompt raised a finger. "Could she have linked the attack to someone removing Aegrino's body?"

"From down here? No idea." I shrugged. "But she's not in the mansion, and if she found something, then it's more of a lead than we've had the whole time." *Maybe we'll catch this killer today, after all.*

"How do we track her?" Gompt looked at me, and in concert, we turned to the pullbeast.

"It's made to follow orders," I said. "I could adjust some of the gearing to process a 'track' command—it will only take a few minutes."

"And I can change the input System to accept a sample of Kratitha's blood." Gompt found a clean rag on a table, and gently mopped up the newest blood stain, absorbing as much as she could into the cloth.

We worked for a time, both engrossed in our respective Symphonies, hearing the overlap in Potential as we changed notes of the same piece, but in different places. Occasionally, the Symphony would resist when we both tried to change notes the same way.

It took another few minutes to restart the Ethulina and align its components, and I felt as if the time added to the weight of my chronograph. It pulled against my vest pocket. Outside, light from the walls of the Nether faded as, inside, lights grew brighter. Each illumination was surrounded by a glow of orange and brown—Systems created from the Houses of Potential and Power.

"Just need to tighten the servos on the neck a bit farther," I told Gompt as I made a half-turn with a screwdriver. "There."

We stepped back. The System Beast had marks on its

flanks that hadn't been there before the attack, and Gompt had installed a device of metal and wood at the pullbeast's neck that could process the music in the cloth containing Kratitha's blood. It wasn't pretty, and we would have to remove our additions before showing it to the Assembly, but it would work.

"I was hoping she'd be back by now," Gompt said, "waltzing in here like a giant honeybee, halfway through our work, telling us how we were wasting our time." The Festuour fiddled her glasses straight again, and wiped oily paws on a rag. There was a streak of grease matting the fur in a line across her chest.

I looked down at my own clothes—still the same ruffled shirt, cravat, and vest I had worn to my interview with the Speaker this morning, though there was a streak of grease across my front where I had leaned over the Ethulina. *I might never get them clean again.* At least I had removed my coat while I worked. I retrieved it from a nearby chair.

"Then we'd best hope this can find her." I reached for the access panel on the neck and flipped a toggle. The System supplying energy completed its circuit, and I danced back as the Ethulina pullbeast sprang to life, snorting and pawing as a real creature would. Neither of us had deactivated the System that made the Beast imitate the genuine animal.

The pullbeast flicked its mane of crystal and snorted dust, then lifted its head as if it smelled something, and trotted out of the room.

Gompt and I scrambled to follow, she tugging her bandolier of pouches tighter, me shrugging into my coat. At least it hadn't attacked us again.

The Ethulina trotted down the corridors, metal hooves clumping on the wood planking. Other maji, still trying to fix broken walls, pipes, and ceilings, shifted to let us past. Given the day's events, it was little wonder a few of them stared.

Our creation led us to the front of the mansion, sniffing at cross-corridors, then through the front doors and down the path to the street. Outside, birds sang quietly in the evening air. The trees on either side cast faint shadows from the dimming walls of the Nether, which stretched far overhead, purple and blue and semi-translucent. I took in a deep breath, grateful for the freshness of the air. The destruction in the mansion had kicked up dust older than I was.

So she did leave. What did Kratitha find?

From outside, the mansion appeared as any other residence belonging to the elite of the Nether, who often chose Poler as a home away from the bustle of the Imperium. Poler had never achieved the greatness of its cousin, though it was in as favorable a position, nestled beneath two of the massive walls that both boxed in and lit the Nether.

The wrought iron gate at the end of the cobbled path separated the mansion from the street, and the Ethulina paused impatiently, one hoof pawing, for me to unlock the gate.

"Gompt, look here," I said, pointing to the carved teak ball, wide as my two hands together, hung from a hook on the central arch above the gate, nestled in a little cup. Metal inlay swirled around it, some hanging just *above* the surface of the object.

The home of the Society was protected from notice by a complex System that influenced anyone approaching into rethinking their path. It had been designed hundreds of cycles ago by a particularly gifted member of the Society. I once spent a ten-day researching it, but gained little insight into how it worked.

One had to turn the sphere off briefly to exit the gate, but the sphere was already dark, inert. Usually it shone to a majus' eyes with all six colors of the houses of the maji.

"Someone's been through here, and one who doesn't care about the secrecy of the Society," Gompt growled.

People will notice a sprawling mansion rising from nothing in a day.

A movement caught my eye. An elderly Lobath was out for a stroll, but he'd dropped the leash to his tentacled pet and was staring toward the mansion.

Oh no. "We need to get the sphere working again, and quickly," I said, rising up on my toes to reach the dull sphere. My hands froze a finger width away from the surface. *That's odd.*

Gompt peered around me. "What is it?"

"The System is still activated," I said.

"But it's off."

"Exactly." I unhooked the sphere entirely from its stand. The Symphony of Potential floated around it, but the music sounded like someone had forgotten to play part of the piece. I couldn't detect the Symphony of Healing, either. I held it out to Gompt, raising my eyebrows in a question.

She cocked her head, as if listening. "The House of Grace isn't a part of the System any longer."

"Something is very broken in this sphere, and it's the only thing keeping out the neighbors." A chill clawed at my chest. *If we can't turn it back on, I don't know who could recreate its protection. Does Moortlin know how? The Society will be exposed even if we find the list!*

Gompt's brow was knotted behind her glasses, and she ran her paws down the pockets of her bandolier. "We need to hurry," was all she said, and my other hand went to my chronograph. A Methiemum woman joined the Lobath in staring at the mansion.

At least it's almost night. Tomorrow morning would be interesting if we couldn't reactivate the sphere, but there was nothing else we could do right now. I put the teak carving back on its perch.

Once the gate was open, the Ethulina sprang forward, making the two spectators leap back. The Lobath tugged at his pet's leash.

"Watch where that thing is going!" the woman yelled.

Now they'll have tales of a mansion rising from nothing, and a mechanical beast that nearly ran them over.

I gritted my teeth, and Gompt and I followed the Ethulina into the quiet city of Poler. Could we fix the sphere before word got too far into the community? Even if we could, the list was still missing, the murderer was still loose, and even if we found them I might be implicated as an accessory.

We jogged around one of the immense columns holding up the ceiling of the Nether, stretching up into the distance. The column's crystal sparkled with the same dim light of the walls. Street lights were coming on, some powered by notes of maji, others simple kerosene lamps. They lit quiet houses, most of their residents already at home. Poler was not known for its nightlife.

These dwellings were familiar. My parents' house was not far away, slightly at an angle to our current path. Walls of stone, and brick rose to both sides of the street. No carriages were in sight, but I doubted we would see many this late.

The Ethulina snorted again and turned down a lane between two large homes. This led to the less affluent sections of the town, and also toward my family's old house. I clenched my fists at my sides. *It belongs to another family now.* I had not been back since a ten-day after the accident, when I removed my family's possessions to a storage facility. They sat there still.

Reaching the end of the lane, the System Beast turned onto the street *toward* my old house, and a surge of something like hot ice rose in my chest. My hands were sweating, though the night was cool.

"Are you well?" Gompt asked. "You're puffing more than the pullbeast."

"It's nothing," I panted, but my eyes were drawn to the stone cottage fourth in a line of similar residences. There was the chipped tile on the roof where I had slipped while climbing when I was seven. There was the branch of the flowering mushfet tree where I used to sit and read.

The damage to the side room has been repaired. There's no reason to look for it.

Gompt restrained the Ethulina and turned to me. "You're white as a ghost. Do you see Kratitha?" Then she followed my gaze. "What's special about that old house—oh."

Suddenly Gompt's paw was on my shoulder, pulling me close to her. The Festuour came from a civilization based on friend groups instead of families. It was natural to her to comfort others when needed.

I'm fine. I don't need anyone else. This pain should be behind me.

I folded into my friend's embrace. The softness of her fur, her firm grip, her musty scent—all pushed reason from my mind, and I felt tears run down my face.

I struggled to reach one hand under my glasses to wipe the offending liquid away, all while Gompt held me close.

"There, there," she said, the nothing words offering far more comfort than they should have. I drew in a deep, ragged breath. Gently, she pushed back to regard me, strong paws gripping my shoulders.

"I'm better," I said, my face hot. The Ethulina was pawing and inching forward despite Gompt's instructions to stay put. "We need to keep moving. Find Kratitha." Gompt nodded and stepped away to let me compose myself.

When we began again, I half expected the System Beast to turn toward my house, as it was where I first came up with the idea of the resonator, but instead it trotted past, as if there were more important things than the end of my youthful innocence.

I looked back several times until we rounded the curve and my parent's home was lost to sight. Why had Kratitha chosen to come this way? Did she know this was my old house or was it just coincidence?

I'll go through that storage facility when this is over.

The Ethulina led us into the heart of Poler, and around another giant column. It supported a market built against the column's side, though the kiosks were empty this time of day.

Finally, with a stamp of what seemed like satisfaction, the pullbeast nosed toward a residence I didn't recognize: neither extravagant, nor poor and tumble-down.

"Kratitha's in here?" I asked, despite knowing it couldn't answer. It stamped a metal hoof again.

Well, maybe it can.

At the door, Gompt shrugged, then raised one paw and knocked.

The door creaked open, and I realized I was staring into the depths of a cowl like those the Sathssn species wore. I was reminded of Tethan, one of those few who eschewed the traditional garments.

"Yes?" The voice sounded female. "This night, there is something you want?"

"We—we're trying to find a friend of ours," I said. *An odd summary of two murders, the chaos at the mansion, and the danger to the Society.* "She's a Pixie, about so high," I put my hand beside my hip. "We have reason to believe she may have...visited this house." I hoped my hesitation wasn't noticeable. I didn't want to accuse every person we talked to of kidnapping.

"Who is at the door, Harha?" called a voice from farther inside the house.

"We're maji, on official business," Gompt put in behind me.

"Maji, they are here from the Imperium," Harha called back.

"We're not—" but I let the words die. I could feel the geas climbing in my mind, stifling any intent to tell them of the mansion or the Society. "We just need to find our friend, and we'll be on our way," I said.

To my surprise, the door opened further. "My mate Slitho and I, we always welcome maji to our home."

"You've met others, then?" Gompt asked.

"Certainly," Harha said. "Though not the one you describe." She wore the usual black boots and gloves of the Sathssn, her cowl pulled forward so only the glint of yellow eyes could be seen. "Us, we are friends with several maji. Usually, we meet them in the Imperium to discuss theology."

Theology? Had we stumbled upon a pair of those who revered the maji as blessed by a divinity? There were groups who still believed that, no matter how much the Council discouraged such thought.

I looked to Gompt, who once again shrugged, though her blue eyes were wide. We would have to be cautious.

"Your...animal...it will have to stay outside," Harha said, looking between us to the Ethulina.

"Not a problem," Gompt said, and flipped the switches for the System Beast to go into an inactive mode. I was confident no one would steal it, as it weighed more than Gompt and me combined.

Inside Slitho and Harha's home, the construction was very plain, the walls consisting of barely-worked wood, with stone blocks set together to make a floor. There was no mortar between them, and several rocked as I stepped on them.

Sections of tree trunk served as chairs, and a slab of wood on another stump was a table. No paintings graced the walls, no rugs on the floor. The hair on my arm lifted in a cool breeze and I realized there was no glass in the windows.

"I have never been in a house...like this," I said. "Is this how people live on Sath Home?" Few who were not Sathssn visited their homeworld.

Why did the Ethulina bring us here?

"This, it is a style little used," Slitho said, as the other resident came through a doorway with no lintel. He held a small bundle of black cloth, which wiggled and gurgled happily. "Only by the Most Traditional of those who serve the Form." I could hear the capitals as he spoke. Slitho had a deep voice for the diminutive species, and I guessed he was used to public speaking. "Please, have a seat. We enjoy conversation with other species and ways of thought."

"'Blasphemers,' he means," Gompt whispered in my ear as we found seats on the unfinished stumps. Mine was of some heavy purple wood, and Gompt chose one that was dull orange with rings of green. We introduced ourselves to the couple.

"We unfortunately have little time for conversation," I said to the two black-cloaked figures. A giggle came from the bundle Slitho held. "Though we would welcome any information on the maji you've spoken with." The openings of their cowls followed me, but aside from that I could tell little of what they looked like. *Have they talked to someone from the Society?*

"This, we understand," Harha said. "Would you care for refreshment while you are here? We have pure water, and a selection of greens from our garden."

"No thanks," Gompt said before I could speak. She was looking at a corner of the room and I saw a bundle of leaves, half separated onto two crude pottery plates.

"I apologize if we've disturbed your meal," I added.

"In this, there is no offense," Slitho said. "We do relish talking with maji. It is our belief they are instrumental in making the Great Assembly a place of happiness and life." He lifted the wiggly bundle he held and I saw two little black footies stick out from underneath. "We wish only the best for our son Essra."

"A noble concept," I said. *Who would disagree with that? Yet why are we here?*

"Me, I am glad you agree." Slitho lifted his son up to stand on one of the Sathssn's thighs. "There is a group of our people who have strong beliefs likewise, and even a few in other species. Too much, we are sick of people rushing around, with no respect. There is murder and crime in the big cities, and people, they are just unkind to each other."

"We wish to celebrate life," Harha said as I fidgeted, wishing to go already. "The maji, they would be a valuable addition to the coalition of likeminded people we know. Devoted, what was the name of the one who came to our house recently? A local majus, I thought." Harha gestured vaguely at her mate.

"The tall fellow, yes," Slitho said, then spoke to Essra in a sing-song voice. "What was his name, now? Lanera? Luni--?"

"Ah, Majus Lunigi," Harha supplied. Both Gompt and I sat bolt upright.

"Majus Aegrino Plumera Lunigi was here?" my friend asked. I leaned forward as if I could pull the answer from them.

"Why—yes," Harha said. If a blank cowl could show surprise, hers did. "You know him? A pleasant Etanela, if a little scattered."

"We are familiar with him." I tried to keep the excitement out of my voice.

"A friend—or was it relation?—of his brought him to one of our meetings," Slitho said. "Majus Lunigi, he found a simple comfort in the things we said. We met with him a few times afterward, as we both lived in Poler. I believe he lives somewhere nearby, though we could never learn quite where."

"With you, we would be happy to share some of the literature our coalition has created," Harha said.

I stood. "Would you mind terribly if I used your facilities?" I asked. "We have been looking for our friend for some time. I'm sure Gompt would be interested in your pamphlets."

"This, it is the least we can do to assist," Slitho said. "Just through there." He pointed to a nearby door, little more than a slab of wood.

I gave Gompt an apologetic grimace as I passed. She showed me her teeth. That was not how Festuour smiled.

I heard her making sounds of agreement as I slipped into the Sathssn couple's bathroom, which was as simple as the rest of their house. The toilet, as I suspected, was merely a hole in the floor covered with a piece of stone.

Kratitha hasn't been in that room, but Aegrino has. So why did the Ethulina track Kratitha here? What's Aegrino's connection to Slitho and Harha? Do they know about Speaker Thurapo's death?

I opened myself to the Symphony of Healing. The melody defining Kratitha's blood was still fresh in my mind. Like any tune, it was simpler to remember a specific section than the whole piece. I found a roll of coarse paper near the toilet, and drew a small knife from my belt.

I winced as I pricked my finger, then squeezed out a single drop of blood onto the paper. The frenetic tempo of my blood slowed as the droplet cooled, and I recreated what I remembered from Kratitha's melody with my own notes, then imposed that refrain over the music in the drop of blood. It was inexact, but until I took my notes back, this droplet would act as Kratitha's blood.

I paced the small room, holding the paper and trying to match the simple tune I constructed with another strand of the Symphony. Outside the door, Gompt's robust tune rolled underneath the counterpoints of Slitho and Harha, with a few trills from Essra. I saw no reason for the pair to lie. They seemed earnest folk, if a little strange.

So why did the System Beast insist Kratitha was here?

There was a little window in the bathroom, also with no glass. I went to it, and a harmony formed with the bloodied paper I held. *Did she only pass close by? If it was close enough, the Ethulina may have been fooled.* I leaned as far out as I could, and the matching music was stronger, down in a curly-leafed bush growing beneath the window. I suspected if it had not been so dark, I might have seen droplets of her blood.

Now I listened to the Symphony of Potential, stroking my beard. The bush had resisted a weight, and I could hear a subtheme playing slower than the rest. Kratitha had been outside this window—for what reason?

Had she been alone? I closed my eyes, listening for where the two Symphonies intersected—where music of biology complemented the energy of bodies. I could almost visualize a corridor of music—Kratitha's path. No...there was another! Someone larger than the diminutive Pixie and me. The music of the other body was quieter. Had she been following the killer?

"Feeling refreshed?" Gompt locked eyes with me as I exited the bathroom. There was a small pile of papers on the stump where I had sat, and the two Sathssn were leaning forward excitedly, while my colleague was turned slightly away. Essra was sitting in her lap, a trail of greenish drool making a slick down his black tunic and matting the fur on Gompt's paw.

"Much better." I looked to the Sathssn. "And I'm sure we've taken up enough of Slitho and Harha's time."

Gompt got to her feet in a flash, handing the little wiggling bundle back to his parents. "Yes. We need to continue searching for Kratitha."

She tried to give a piece of paper back to Slitho as well, but he waved her away. "This information, keep it. If you feel inclined to come to one of our meetings, we are always accepting of new members."

We made our farewells, and exited. Gompt reactivated the System Beast, and we walked down the front path. I could see Gompt's furry ears quivering with the effort of not saying anything.

"Kratitha passed by the side of their house," I said. "We should be able to pick up her trail the next street over."

"Then maybe listening to that gibberish while you played around in the bathroom was worth it," Gompt growled. "'Coalition who believe in life' indeed. I wouldn't be surprised if they were trying to gouge maji out of their money. It all sounds very inexact and fluffy." She shook her head disgustedly.

"Many religions sound like that," I countered. "Though I can't say what Aegrino saw in it. I thought he was a logical individual. It feels like this should be connected to the Speaker's murder, but I have no idea how."

We turned a corner, the pullbeast trotting along behind us. "On top of that, Kratitha stopped by their bathroom window."

"Why?" Gompt asked. "Did she figure out Aegrino went to listen to those two fanatics?"

I shook my head, then pushed my glasses back up. "Unknown. Maybe she saw a chance to bandage her wounds."

Gompt shook her head. "The way Kratitha's mind skids like a cub on ice, she'd probably forgotten she was bleeding by that point. She must have been looking for something, or someone."

I acknowledged the point with a wave of a hand. "Then what did she know? Why did she leave, and why didn't she tell us about it?"

"The mansion *was* exploding at the time." Gompt rested a hand on the pullbeast's flank. It was pulling ahead, leaning into the next turn. The System Gompt had attached to its throat must have picked up Kratitha's trail again.

"What is the connection between Kratitha and Aegrino?" Gompt mused. "I don't know if they'd even talked to each other." I could just see her questioning blue eyes in the twilight from the walls of the Nether.

"She was following someone," I repeated. "Or was it the other way around? Kratitha might have been captive, and tried to call for help at that house." The pullbeast was slowing, and we slowed with it. "If the killer has my invention, they can cause catastrophe with any Systems they encounter." I paused. "What is it?"

Gompt was peering into one of the System Beast's hatches, one paw scrabbling for a set of gears. "It's stopped. Something must be wrong."

"Uh, Gompt," I said. *I hope that isn't...* "Gompt!"

My colleague jerked up. "What? Oh—is that—?"

We ran to the entrance of a nearby alley, where a small lump of clothes and wings lay in a pile.

I put one hand under Kratitha's neck, staring into her face. Her compound eyes never closed, and Pixies rarely slept—a product of their short life cycle—so if one was unconscious, it was a bad sign.

"Is she still with us?" Gompt put a paw on the Pixie's arm, her neck, then let out a frustrated snort. "No circulatory system, or at least no pulse to feel. How do you tell if a Pixie's alive if it's not running around?"

"By how much talking they do," Kratitha said in a weak voice, and Gompt and I exhaled in relief. She pushed up on one hand, her wings starting to buzz. We scooted back to give her more room.

"Why did you leave the mansion?" I asked. "What happened to you?"

Kratitha waved one hand at me, the other running over the chitinous ridges that decorated the top of her head. "Must have hit me harder than I thought." She got to her feet, wings lifting her.

"Someone hit you? Who?" Gompt had her paws out to catch the Pixie if she fell.

Kratitha looked between us. "Thought you were smarter than that. Aegrino, of course. He stole your invention I fixed, Mandamon."

PART SIX

Harmonic

- Many think Pixies are dumb beasts, hardly worthy to be allowed entrance into Great Assembly. This is false. Pixies are varied and individual as other species, though we come from hive mind mentality. Few visit Mother Hive to see firsthand. This is part of reason warrior-descended hives can wage war without oversight from Great Assembly. First to go were philosophical and religious-descended hives, dating back from original five-mother split over twenty-five hundred cycles previous. Warriors needed scientists and engineers for many cycles, but now think they can get progress from trading with other species. Instinct to kill off cousin hives grows overwhelming in warrior hives. I fear my generation may be last of forward thinkers on Mother Hive.

On the genocide of Mother Hive, by Kratithakanipouliteka, Pixie majus of the Houses of Power and Grace

"Aegrino's alive?" I asked, aghast. I had listened to his Symphony degrade, felt his dead wrist, and seen the bloody wounds in his chest.

"Can't be," Gompt said. "We both checked him out. Deader than a furry scrounger in a trap."

"Saw him come out of records room," Kratitha said. Now she was upright, her wings were buzzing like a swarm of insects, lifting her shoes up off the pavement. She brushed mud off her shirt. "Brought the Ethulina with you? Gompt modified the initiative System to replace with tracking. Could fix that so it does both, with time." Kratitha half-floated toward the pullbeast. "Had your invention when he left the records room.

Must have caused all the System input errors in the mansion."

I took a moment to process her stream of information. She must have been feeling better. "Wait—you saw Aegrino with the harmonic resonator? My resonator?" My mind raced. "Then did he kill the Speaker after all? Did he clean up the body or not? If not, Thurapo's secretary must have found the body by now." *Or did Aegrino kill her too? Another Etanela murdered?*

"Was very much alive." Kratitha had reached the System Beast and opened a hatch. "Hm. Gears in back left flank are blunted. Probably from shock, walking on cobblestone. Or maybe from fight in mansion. Need stronger heat treat for production models." She turned back. "Followed him for a while, but figured out I was there. Ambushed me in alley." She raised one thin finger to the dark side street where we had found her. A single streetlight illuminated her face.

"Hold on just a dang moment," Gompt said. She squinted down at the Pixie. "You said you *fixed* Mandamon's invention?"

I blinked and reviewed Kratitha's stream of words. She talked so fast it was sometimes hard to keep track of everything. "So *you* stole it out of my cabinet?" I asked.

Kratitha's feet landed firmly on the ground, her wings drooping. "Thought I could increase efficiency, make use of it in System Beast project to coordinate different sub-Systems. Increased operating range, but, ah, you know that."

Gompt snapped her furry fingers. "That's how Aegrino could affect the entire mansion at once."

"After he was dead, I might add, which is the more impressive part of it." I looked up at the single streetlight, its light glinting off the metal of the Ethulina's hooves. It was one of the majus-fueled ones. *There's still something that doesn't add up.* "How did Aegrino get hold of the resonator wand, if you had it?" I asked.

Kratitha shrugged. "Found it in the workshop? Meant to tell you about it, but kept slipping my mind."

"He must have picked it up before last night. The Speaker was killed early this morning." The messy cut through the Speaker's throat was similar to the slices in Aegrino's chest. "But then how did he fake his death? Those wounds were lethal."

"He was...is a Dancer—Communication and Grace," Gompt said. "Both houses can be subtle. Maybe we didn't actually see what we thought we did."

Kratitha's wings were buzzing again. "House of Grace could couple with Communication to mask signs of life? Breath?"

"Could be." Now Gompt looked thoughtful. "Neither of us hears Communication, but I've heard talk it's good for messing with what others hear or say."

"Grace musical component acts as helping component. Increases efficiency. Smooths flaws." Kratitha suggested, the light reflecting off her compound eyes.

I put my hands on my hips. "So, he dulled his vital signs with the House of Grace, and interfered with us detecting them with Communication," *Why pretend to be dead in the first place?* "Could he have conjured up great slashes in his chest? Those looked—and felt—pretty fatal." I looked at my hands. "If I hadn't sterilized and cleaned my fingers after touching the body, I could test for fakery with the Symphony of Healing. Too late now."

The others were silent.

"You're sure it was Aegrino? Not another Etanela?" I

asked Kratitha. There were a suspicious number of the tall species involved.

She buzzed her wings, lifting off the ground for a moment. "Had the harmonic resonator, very tall, came from records room, saw blood on front of shirt, golden hair, yes? Who else?"

I stroked my beard. "Aegrino was very convincingly surprised when we told him Speaker Thurapo was dead. He even seemed to know Thurapo. Said he had to tell his sister."

"House of Communication again?" Gompt asked. "So, Aegrino's better at lying than being a record keeper." She pushed up her glasses and glanced around the dim intersection. "Though that still doesn't explain why he would steal his own list, give it to the Speaker, then kill him."

Kratitha's wings trembled above her head, a sign of nervousness. "Two Etanela victims. Some species rivalry? Or blackmail to steal list." She turned away from us and toward the pullbeast, running a hand down its flank.

Why is she nervous? Is she scared she followed a murderer?

"Moortlin mentioned a specist crime." Gompt ran a hand across her belt of tools, as if to check they were all there. "It's right weird. I can't see how murder has anything to do with a missing list of Society members."

"Maybe Aegrino found way around geas by communication with another member of species?" Kratitha suggested. She was still turned away.

"I've never been able to do anything like that," I said, "and I've talked to plenty of Methiemum."

"Also not House of Communication," Kratitha said.

"One way to find out." I stood beside the Pixie and

opened the hatch at the Ethulina's neck. I set it to follow us. If Aegrino was the murderer, we'd need all the help we could get against another two-house majus. I also took the time to watch Kratitha. She was trembling, but I'd only caught it because I was looking for it.

What is going on with her?

"We need to find Aegrino quickly." I said. "If he's found a way around the geas, and wants to bring down the Society, it will ruin any chance we have of bringing the System Beasts to market."

"And any other inventions after," Gompt added. "Might even harm other products invented in the Society."

"Didn't see where he went after was hit." Kratitha gestured around the dim streets. "Which direction?"

The single streetlight overhead went out with a crack of glass.

"Gompt? Kratitha?" Their queries greeted me, and heard the scrape of metal on rock as the Ethulina moved a hoof. The Nether's walls, towering over Poler, provided faint light, but only enough to see shapes, once my eyes adjusted.

Wings buzzed, and I felt a gust as Kratitha flitted by. "Saw movement over here," she said. Pixie eyes must adjust to light changes quicker. Aegrino might not have gone that far after all.

Gompt and I groped after our colleague's voice. "Can't see a blamed thing," Gompt muttered. The *ping* and *clop* of hooves sounded behind. The pullbeast was following.

"Gompt, number four spanner," Kratitha called, and I heard the Festuour fumble in one of her pouches. There was a *whizz* in the air in front of us, and something clattered, farther down an alley.

"Kratitha, did you throw my *best spanner*?" Gompt's voice was a low growl.

"Missed him too," Kratitha said. She seemed unaffected by the growl that put the hairs on my arms on end. *Maybe Pixies don't have a large evolutionary predator covered with fur.*

"We'll get it back," I said quickly. "Won't we, Kratitha?"

"Yes yes," she said. "This way. Might be good time to listen to Symphony?"

My eyes were adjusting, stone walls passing on both sides as we rattled down the streets of Poler. I heard Gompt grunt and sweep something from the ground.

"The shaft's nicked," she grumbled at Kratitha's wings.

"Will buff it out later," Kratitha called back. "Trying to listen to connections in House of Power. Might be trying to flank."

The Symphonies of Potential and Healing were a chaotic arpeggio of changing energy. Kratitha was a fugue of notes—a master belting out a constantly changing stream of rhythm. Gompt was a lower, solid beat with a rumbling base line driving forward. I tuned out the mechanical repetition of the pullbeast, as there was another theme, buried underneath the top layer of music. This contained long, languid sweeps of melody, increasing and decreasing in pitch. Was that Aegrino? I tried to remember what I had heard around his body, but it had been too long ago.

"He's going left," I called, and we swerved onto a side street where a few lights still shone. These were kerosene, not powered by maji.

We pulled to a stop, but the Ethulina sped past, as if seeking revenge for being made to fight its creators. At the end of the street, back to a wall, was a tall figure, certainly an Etanela. He was holding a long object.

My resonator!

The resonator flashed in the air, and the pullbeast jerked, its feet tumbling over each other. It sprawled in the grass, just a pile of connected limbs. Rage built in me. There was too much time invested in the System Beast for Aegrino to destroy it.

"Don't let him hurt it more!" Gompt cried. She must have been thinking the same as I was. "Careful—he's got Communication and Grace."

"Can handle Grace," Kratitha said, flying forward toward the prone pullbeast.

Below her, the street ruptured, throwing cobbles in all directions. I shielded my face with an arm, but could hear the deep *thump* of the stones hitting grass, and the patter of water falling down in a shower.

When I looked again, a blue glow surrounded broken clay pipes, poking up from the street. Water puddled around it. Aegrino had used my invention to make the System in a water pipe go haywire. My teeth ground together at the misuse, the casual destruction.

Kratitha was on the ground, one wing bent back, a ragged piece missing from the top. A cobble must have grazed her. She reached an arm behind her to assess the damage.

Gompt and I rushed forward together, but skidded to a halt as the air flashed like glass, reflecting dim light back toward the walls and streetlights. Gompt yelled and clapped a hand to her side.

"What was that?" I called. The glass-like reflection in the air was gone, and I swiveled side to side, trying to see if there was anything left. There had been a sting of sound in the Symphonies—both Symphonies—when it happened.

"Don't come closer," Aegrino called out, his voice was nervous in the clear night air, higher than the record keeper's usual timbre. His mop of golden hair wavered like a cloud above his head as he checked the dead end behind him. There wasn't much light, but I thought I could see dark blotches on his shirt. With the wounds I'd seen, I had no idea how he was standing.

"Give me back the harmonic resonator," I called out "And the list of—" my mouth rebelled at me and that annoying jingle of music played, scattering my thoughts. "The names you have." *He'll know what I mean.*

"I'm afraid I can't." Aegrino's words slurred together, as Etanela's speech did when they were excited. "This is the only way to keep you maji from doing more harm. This is an excellent weapon to reveal your secrets."

Kratitha yelled and dove forward, but she was slow. What was left of her left wing membrane trembled, not in concert with the right. Aegrino turned the wand toward her and pushed a button. Another splash of sound played through my head.

"Stop, Kratitha!" I called, but it was too late. The slivers of light appeared again, right in front of the Pixie and she screamed, falling back. Brown blood splattered on the Ethulina, and trickled down Kratitha's arms and front.

"Best not to rush in here," Gompt said, to my left. "Aegrino's a trained majus. He's skilled in the Symphonies of Communication and Grace, so why ain't he using them? Why is he talking about the maji like that? Wasn't his shirt a different color when we found him 'dead?'"

It's not Aegrino?

"I'm getting past you," the figure said. "Don't follow me, or I'll carve you up, maji or not!"

"Don't know if even the House of Grace can avoid those spikes of nothingness," Gompt said. "Do you hear that resonance in the Symphony too?"

I stared back. "I thought it was just me. It must be creating a feedback loop between the notes—"

I broke off. *Just like the accident.* In a split second, the memory pushed through my mind, as my hand went to the scar around my eye.

It was after dinner in my parent's home. I showed my mentor, Abarham, how the resonator created a connection between different Systems, causing them to work in tandem. But the harmonics multiplied out of control. Walls caved in. I smelled blood and dust as a chunk of the roof crushed Abarham in front of me. A rafter nearly put out my eye.

I crawled from the wreckage, but my parents didn't. When the Poler City Guard and the Fire Brigade arrived, they found lacerations on all three bodies. I had cuts all down my arms.

The resonances my invention made in the Symphony were so concentrated, they intruded into physical space. I'd never made the connection before, but now I did, my mind flashing through the wand's construction.

"I know how to stop the resonator," I told Gompt. I looked to Kratitha. She was holding hands over her arms, and blood was running down her front. "But it will take all three of us."

"Move aside! Leave me in peace!" the figure yelled. He was trapped, with the stone wall behind him, but he'd stopped our attack with almost no effort. We couldn't let him leave. "My friends and I won't bother you."

"Friends without *two houses*," Gompt called back, getting around the geas' restraints.

"Not maji at all." Aegrino/not-Aegrino backed up,

my wand held in front of him. "Just a coalition of like-minded people. We're trying to make the Assembly a better place, but you people had to bring Juristo into this—blackmail him!"

"Who?" I had no idea who this Juristo was, and I met Gompt's eyes, then Kratitha's multifaceted orbs. Had they heard the same thing?

"On the way here," Kratitha gasped out. She was crouched low. The top of her left wing was a mess of crumpled tissue. Like butterflies or bees, I didn't know if Pixie's wings ever healed. "Heard things while Aegrino—or this person," she jerked a thumb toward our antagonist, "spoke to weird Sathssn."

"We found the place," Gompt said. "Slitho and Harha, right?" The Pixie cocked her head at us, then nodded.

"It was to protect Juristo! You didn't even know his name?" Aegrino/not-Aegrino called. "Back away and we can all leave in peace." The figured shuffled his feet back and forth, as if he were about to run between us. I wasn't going to let that happen.

"You've murdered another Etanela," I shouted back. "Maybe two. We'll track you anywhere you go."

A shift in the figure's stance told me he'd decided to attack again rather than run at us, so I was ready this time when he pushed a button. He knew how to use the resonator, but I guessed he didn't know everything, especially if Kratitha had tinkered with it.

The wave of harmonics was like a pipe organ overriding the Symphony, all notes tuned to the same key, playing concert. It pushed into the Symphonies of Healing and Potential, and disturbances in the air reflected the faint light from the streetlight and fading walls of the Nether, traveling toward us like shards of thrown glass.

They'll slice us to ribbons. Don't have time to explain the change using all three of us.

I did the best I could with an instant's thought.

The notes in the Symphony of Potential were overwhelmed with the harmonics, and I took notes from my being to change them, bridge the gaps, and let those powerful chords become part of my being. I absorbed the energy into myself, knowing it would rip my bones apart and shred my muscles. Fortunately I had more than one house.

The Symphony of Healing was a riot of disruptions, Gompt and Kratitha's notes unraveling despite me taking the brunt of the attack. As if in slow motion, I could see fur separating on Gompt's torso, skin tearing.

I took more notes from my being, and altered the monoliths of noise, bridging from melody to melody in the Symphony of Healing, dispersing the harmonics between different branches of music.

I was dimly aware that I was on my knees. The energy I had taken in with the Symphony of Potential threatened to shake me apart. I stole yet more notes from the melody that made up my being, dispersing the energy. My fingers felt like they were on fire, my heart hammering. Kratitha screamed, and out of the corner of my eye I saw a line of brown open from her forearm to wrist.

I won't let what happened to Abarham and my parents happen again.

I took more of the resonance into myself, breaking it into component notes, changing tempo and key so they could no longer harmonize. I could not reclaim these notes, and it would take many days to rebuild my song.

I shook, pitching forward, then realized the wall of sound had ceased.

I raised my head. My eyesight was blurry, my hands trembling, as if I had touched one of the live wires transmitting electricity to the new lights in the mansion.

"What? You should be dead!" Not-Aegrino was adjusting settings on my device. "It was an accident before, but I remember. I remember."

I waved my shaking hands at my friends to come closer so I could explain. Gompt was bleeding from her chest, but the cuts were shallow. Kratitha was in worse shape, but the little Pixie limped over, her head high.

"Must keep resonant harmonics from—ow—from forming," she said.

"That's right." My shaking was subsiding. "The harmonic resonator combines available melodies into a harmony. If prevented, I believe the energy will feed back into the device."

"You believe?" Gompt said. Her voice was raw.

"It's the best chance we have," I said, watching the figure standing at the end of the street. "Listen to your Symphonies. Keep the melodies from harmonizing. It will be hard, but we only need to hold the changes for a few seconds. We can try—" I broke off, seeing the other figure look up. "No time. Get ready."

The others spun around, as not-Aegrino raised the wand. I could already hear strands of the Symphony of Potential wavering, tones speeding or slowing to fall into a rhythm. I took more notes from my song. *It's so bare of music.* The notes would return over time, but it would take many more experiences for me to grow back to my full potential.

I inserted my notes like bookmarks between pages, keeping them from sticking together. This was not a carefully crafted change, but creating music with no theme, stuffing notes into both Symphonies that did not belong in the beautiful, natural music of the universe. I could hear Gompt doing the same thing in the Symphony of Potential.

Auras surrounded the three of us in the colors of our houses, visible only to another majus, blue and brown for Gompt, white and brown around me, and blue and orange around Kratitha. Sparks filled the air, dancing off motes of dust, and blinding me for a moment. I heard a crack of stone, and a twisting, splintering noise of wood exploding. Seconds later, I turned my head away as tiny slivers pelted my face, dropping away harmlessly.

When my vision returned, a line of cobbles in front of me was fractured. The streetlight danced with flame, the entire globe around the light engulfed in fire. A nearby bush was wilted, dropping leaves, and Gompt's fur shone with ice.

"It worked!" Gompt called, and I looked up. The figure was braced against the wall, my invention a shredded mess. Even from this distance, I could see splinters of wood and metal imbedded in his bluish hands. More blood dotted his shirt, where slivers had driven into his chest.

Gompt rushed forward, past the prone System Beast, and I followed, puffing as if I had raced across Poler. Kratitha came behind, but she was slow, obviously hurting.

Our antagonist struggled up, but Gompt got there first, checking the other person with a massive shoulder. He staggered against the wall and Gompt clamped both furry paws—strong from months of crafting in the workshop—on his arms.

I looked up into the Etanela's face. It *was* Aegrino, except it wasn't. The face was subtly different, but also familiar. The hair was the same shade, and in the same style.

I know this person.

This was a dominate female of the Etanela, while Aegrino had been a subordinate male—two of the four divisions of Etanela gender.

Bloody slashes marked her chest as they had Aegrino, though in this case not fatally. Had it happened at the same time? I imagined the resonator between the two, creating deadly energy and slashing at both Etanela. Slashing at the Speaker's neck.

She was wearing makeup before. That's why I didn't recognize her similarity to Aegrino.

"You're the secretary!" I said. My voice was like sandpaper. I might have screamed while the resonant notes coursed through my body. "How do you know about the...the Society?" The geas let me whisper the word. This person clearly knew more than she should.

"I heard a lot, as a secretary to one of the Assembly's speakers," she muttered. "I just needed to get you out of the way so I could clean up. I knew you wouldn't go to the Imperium guard."

The Etanela's hands did not describe fluid patterns, as normal for the species. Instead she held them in front of her, trembling as she tried to prize shards of wood from where they punctured her palms. Greenish blood dripped, and I could see the tips of several splinters poking all the way through the backs of her blue-tinted hands.

"Did you kill Aegrino?" Gompt said, still holding the Etanela's arms. Kratitha stared up to meet our prisoner's eyes.

"My name is Bethaya Plumire Lunigi," she said. Her voice shook, the words slurring together so much it was difficult to understand her.

"Related to Aegrino, by the name," Kratitha croaked, and Bethaya nodded, her mane of hair waving.

"He was my brother—great Sea Mother, it was an accident!" Bethaya wailed. "Everything went so fast. We were just supposed to disrupt the geas with this—thing." She lifted her hands, where the shards of the resonator pierced her.

Aegrino said he had to tell his sister about Speaker Thurapo's death. But she already knew. His sister was *the secretary...*

"Then you are aware of the Society," Gompt rumbled.

"I've known for cycles," Bethaya said. Tears were flowing down her face. "Slitho and Harha were the ones to finally understand, of all the people my brother and I have tried to tell." Words flowed from her, as if from a deflating balloon. "We used your accident as an example of the dangers of the Society. Aegrino learned about the resonator wand from his records, then glimpsed it in your workshop one day." Kratitha hissed in air at that.

What are those two Sathssn up to? "Was Speaker Thurapo an accident too?" I asked. "Were you trying to recruit a speaker to your cause?"

I did not expect Bethaya's next response, which was to crumple to the ground. Gompt barely kept hold on the Etanela's limp arms.

"Sea Mother. It had just happened when I heard you coming. I had no time to take care of Juristo's body." Bethaya looked at me, seated on the cobbles of Poler, face wet with tears.

Juristo is *Speaker Thurapo.* It was like a sheet of cold water washed over me. I hadn't known his given name.

Bethaya must have been with the Speaker before I got there this morning. *Her eyes weren't puffy from sleep this morning—they were puffy from* crying. Things began to fall into place.

"More than a secretary to Thurapo, yes?" Kratitha asked.

Bethaya sunk in farther, and I her response was almost inaudible. "Juristo and I...became intimate. That Benish councilor pressured him to listen to your proposal, or they would tell Juristo's mates about us." Bethaya's words trailed off in a sob.

"Then...*you're* the leverage the Society had on the Speaker." I said. "Finally, some motive to interfere with the System Beast proposal, and the Society."

"He had been studying that accursed list of names all night," Bethaya said. "I thought this was finally the chance Harha and I talked about, to show someone in power how our Life Coalition thought."

"Wait—you didn't give him the list of Society names?" Gompt asked, and I stared at our captive. Something *still* didn't fit. Kratitha hunched in, and her compound eyes took in everything.

Bethaya slowly pulled a splinter from her palm, hissing in pain. "No. Juristo said someone delivered the list the night before—a Pixie. I saw the chance to show him what destruction two-house maji can cause." She looked up at me suddenly, venomous. "Even if you make people forget about the explosion you caused in Poler, others won't. But they don't know about the Society. I do. I can show how its members play with forces beyond their control."

"That was an—an accident," I choked out, mirroring Bethaya's excuse. "My parents *died*, as did my mentor.

You have no right to—" I stopped at Gompt's hand on my arm.

"We'll figure that out later," she said.

Had I been yelling? My hands were in tight fists.

Bethaya was talking about how the Speaker wanted a demonstration, and how it went wrong, but I had seen those effects for myself, and Thurapo had paid the ultimate price.

My eyes were on Kratitha, hunched beside me. She was no longer looking in my direction.

There were plenty of Pixies in the Society. Fewer than my species, but a good handful. It could have been any of them who delivered the list to the Speaker. But Kratitha had already admitted to adjusting my invention. An invention which Aegrino thought could remove the geas.

"Did you—" I started, but as usual, my colleague was ahead of me.

"Did not anticipate these events," Kratitha said, still hunched over. Her right hand cradled her left arm, tracing around the sliced skin running the length of her forearm, still slowly leaking blood. "Had separate reasons to talk to the Speaker. My caste needs protection. Few scientists left, even now. A genocide, by the warrior caste, and Speaker had...requirements. He suspected Society existed and wanted independent proof. Found a way to accommodate. Promised would not go farther than him."

"You little maggot," Gompt spat. Now it was my turn to put a restraining arm out. "You could have told us at any time where the list of members came from, but you let us wander around like fools."

"For our good," Kratitha said, and her voice gained strength, and speed. "For the good of the System Beasts. The Speaker would approve vote—get other Etanela to vote our way. Would send support to family on Mother Hive. Didn't know about this one when I did it." The Pixie waved a languid hand toward Bethaya.

"Too many secrets," I said. I pulled Bethaya to her feet, keeping a tight hold on her. I trusted Kratitha to come along with us. She may have been misguided, but I knew her well enough to know her loyalties aligned with ours. There would be...complications. "Where is Aegrino's body?" I asked our prisoner.

"Burned," she said. "As is Juristo's. Sea Mother, what have I done?" She sank again, but Gompt and I supported her.

"She's in shock," I said. "Let's get back to the mansion, and figure this out properly."

"It was *your* weapon that did this," Bethaya snarled, and I deflected a half-serious swipe at my head.

"An *invention*," I replied, "and one that has constructive uses. There was a reason I broke it."

"Apologies," Kratitha mumbled, shuffling along beside us. I could tell she was in pain. It might dull her hyperactive nature until Gompt and I reached Moortlin to tell them what had happened.

I went to the heap of the Ethulina, and was surprised to find the Systems still intact, but jumbled. I used a precious few more of my notes to knit the aspect back together, and our creation wobbled to its front hooves, then up on all fours. It followed us, favoring a rear leg.

At least the System Beasts are innocent in all this. We still need to get their production approved, somehow.

"How much do these Sathssn know?" I asked Bethaya as we walked. "Will they be a problem for the Society?"

The Etanela grunted as she pulled another shard from her hand, leaving the splinter beside the road. I watched it fall behind us. *Maybe I can make a version that works as intended.*

"Slitho and Harha are innocent," Bethaya said. "Leave them out of this."

"They know about the Society," Gompt said. A line of red marred her chest fur.

"So do I," Bethaya said. "So do the families of the maji who are members. Leave the Sathssn's Life Coalition out of this. It's a small collection of like-minded people who merely want the universe to be a better place."

I snorted, and Gompt rumbled a growl. That didn't match what Bethaya said about maji having too much power. It was also a common complaint, and I'd endured enough of the Sathssn's trite nonsense to know it was a fad like other intersections of religion and philosophy dotting the Great Assembly. If the Life Coalition was so concerned with making everyone happy, and with recruiting majus members, the little group wouldn't do anything against the influence of the maji.

The Society of Two Houses

- My great-grandfather Slithen, you know him as 'the Dreamer.' This, it is a title given after his series of still-unexplained visions, thought to be sent by the Ideal Form itself. Our coalition of believers, who celebrate the beauty of life perfected, came into existence over fifteen cycles after his death, when I was an infant. For cycles, we have languished, slowly growing our membership, and recently even reaching out to blasphemers outside our species. Me, I am happy to report plans for a new invention delivered by one of these outsiders. I hope this will put to rest discord of whether other species should be included. Information about this invention will speed the work of our scientists and maji in discovering the method to pierce the shroud between our universe and the beyond.

Notes of Harha to select members of the Most Traditional Servant sect of the Cult of Form, 953 A.A.W.

We reached the mansion as the light of the walls brightened. I had been awake a long time, starting early yesterday morning when I found the Speaker dead.

Bethaya came along quietly, neither trying to escape nor fighting our guiding hands. She had lost a brother and a lover in one day, by her own misguided hand.

I lost parents and mentor in one day, too. She will remember this for the rest of her life.

Kratitha trudged along, her damaged wing unable to carry her weight. She spoke little—a sign of how cowed she was.

We passed the gates of the mansion, and I looked to

the sphere containing the inert concealing System. It was yet another problem the Society would need to fix, along with the damage to the interior of the mansion.

We must have been a sight. Even amidst the chaos we drew the gazes of other Society members as we climbed the mansion's main staircase. Plithin A'Tyf and his spouses were cleaning fallen ceiling plaster, and the trio of Lobath nodded to us gravely. Plithin looked as if he might speak, but we hurried past.

Moortlin was in their study, and at our knock, I heard the click of multiple latches being drawn.

The door creaked open and the head of the Society took us all in with one sweep of his unblinking yellow eyes, then gestured into his office. We crowded in, and Moortlin bolted the door again, ensuring we would not be disturbed.

"Bethaya," he said to the Etanela, with a creak of his head. "One remembers there was a ban in effect to keep this one from entering the mansion. Does this one need to be escorted out again?"

"Then you know her?" Gompt said. She took a step toward the Benish. "You could have mentioned she was Thurapo's lover."

Moortlin raised one thick hand out to the side. "One was not aware that one was, hm, even involved, nor could enter the mansion. Bethaya is, hm, the one this group searched for? How would that one get the list, and what of Speaker Thurapo? One visited the Dome of the Assembly, but Aegrino had already, hm, cleaned up the body and the Speaker's office."

"Bethaya was the one who took care of both bodies— burned them," I told the Benish. I spared a look at Kratitha, who must have caught my movement, though her head was bowed. Her assent was a quick twitch of her head. "Though it turns out Bethaya was not involved with the disappearance of the list of Society members."

It was the closest I had seen to Moortlin being surprised. Their eyes blinked dim, then back to their normal luminescence, both hands coming up and out, as if reaching for the answer. "There are more here who wish to see the, hm, Society gone?" they asked. "One suspected the Society would fragment again—one's enemies have increased over the last two hundred cycles."

I was saved having to explain by Kratitha. "Was a matter of family," she said. "Of caste and pride, and—and Speaker Thurapo asked for much in return for support from Etanela fighters. He suspected Society existed."

Moortlin's head turned from side to side, creaking like a door in need of oil. "The Council of the Maji has been concerned with the recent hostilities between the warrior and scientist classes on Mother Hive. One was surprised when the latest reports said the warriors were beginning to, hm, lose battles." They reached a hand out toward the little Pixie. "This one had an involvement in that situation?"

Kratitha raised her head. "Was birthed in the new scientist queen's first brood. Only majus among them, and close to queen mother. She insisted something be done. Wouldn't agree to any truce with the warrior mother. Reached out offworld through me. Speaker Thurapo insisted on information in return for help."

"This one could speak or write of the Society?" Moortlin's words were quiet, but I could discern the edge of tension—or was it panic?

"Turns out Mandamon's invention could disrupt the geas, with a little tweaking," Gompt said from where she was helping Bethaya remove more splinters of my wand from her hand. The two were leaving green bloodstains on Moortlin's carpet. "Kratitha got her hands on it before Bethaya stole it. Aegrino must have given it to her to try to disrupt the geas around them, too." The Festuour held up one of Bethaya's hands as the Etanela nodded, confirming Gompt's theory. "It won't be a problem any longer."

Moortlin shook their head with a dull creak. "No. Once a secret has been breached, hm, it is far easier to breach again." They made a fist. "One has already had an inquiry about the mansion, now the System at the gates has been damaged. One assumes this is also Bethaya's work?" The Etanela didn't answer, and Moortlin continued.

"Mandamon knows the construction of the instrument, Kratitha a way to modify the Symphony attached to it. If a dire need arose, could any of this group swear not to make another object to, hm, render the geas inoperative?"

None of us could meet the Benish's eyes.

"One thought not." They watched Bethaya picking at the shards of my invention, and their voice lessened from sandpaper over wood to a file on leather. "Bethaya. Bethaya!" The Etanela looked up, obviously still in shock. Her eyes did not focus on the Benish. "This one has the, hm, copy of the list of Society members? This one took it from the Speaker's study, yes?"

Slowly, Bethaya nodded. "I did," she said. "But after what happened to Aegrino, I...I," she stopped again, staring into the distance.

"What did you do with it?" I urged her, and she watched me as if she didn't remember who I was. "The list?"

Her head came up, looking to the ceiling of Moortlin's study. "I burned the salt-soaked thing, with their bodies."

Moortlin made a low noise; the creak of an oak settling after a hurricane. "Not ideal. One would like to, hm, have the list in hand rather than supposedly burned and gone." They sighed. "If this is the situation, then this group will make the best of it." They turned to Gompt. "Please take Bethaya to the clinical ward. That one's wounds must be treated before, hm, a trial is attempted."

Gompt looked like she might say something, but Moortlin's stern expression cut her off. She nodded, and helped Bethaya rise, still picking wood and metal shards from her hands. Gompt unlocked several clasps and chains on the door before it would open. Moortlin locked it behind her. They put their back to the door. "Kratitha, this one made no other copies of the list?"

The Pixie shook her head. "Stole the one Aegrino copied, then took it to the Speaker. Only because Mother was in danger. Would never hurt the Society otherwise."

I cocked my head. *Something isn't right.* "But the Speaker copied at least part of the list. I picked up the indentations on his writing pad. Neither list was in the room."

"As one said," Moortlin replied. "When a secret is, hm, revealed, it is very difficult to conceal it again."

Kratitha looked between the two of us holding her arm. Her stooped stance spoke of bone-deep tiredness. "Delivered the list to Speaker very early in morning—previous night, really. Speaker copies list. Then Bethaya shows invention to Speaker and Speaker shows her copy?" She swayed just slightly before her intact wing buzzed to support her. "Yet Bethaya only takes copy, burns it, and Mandamon finds nothing." She paused as if we should be able to fill in the missing information. "Only two solutions. Either paper still hidden in Speaker Thurapo's study, or another person took it."

Moortlin clenched their hands with a creak like wood about to snap. I took an involuntary step back. "It may be impossible to save the Society from the breach, as, hm, one has already stated." They opened their hands again, and their eyes brightened.

They stepped away from the door. "Kratitha, follow the others. This one also needs medical attention, and has a presentation to show off the, hm, System Beast. This group will need to be fully healed."

"But the Speaker—," I started.

"Presentation not yet approved," added Kratitha, even as she loosened latches. It was a sign of her discomfort that she didn't protest the Benish's order.

"One has made, hm, other arrangements." Moortlin said. "It is not preferable. It leaves a trail connecting the System Beast to one, to the Society, and to the mansion. At this point, the truth is perhaps, hm, unavoidable."

"What of punishment?" Kratitha ventured.

Moortlin waggled their fingers. "Much has been done in the Society by suspect means for the good of the whole. One is glad this one's caste has a chance to survive. The Assembly needs more scientists, and fewer warriors."

"Thank you," Kratitha whispered, before pulling the door closed behind her.

As soon as we were alone, Moortlin creaked to the door, pulling latches locked once again. I wondered if they could save time and dispense with the action, but they finished quickly, and took three straight-legged strides to their desk.

"Moortlin?" I asked, but the Benish fished something from deep in a pile of paper on their desk with a grunt, and passed it over.

It was a list of Society members.

But this was lost. Someone took it. "Is this—? Did you—?"

"Buried in the bottom, locked drawer of Speaker Thurapo's desk." I was almost certain Moortlin's craggy face showed a smile, though I don't think I'd ever seen that expression on them. "Bethaya thought the copy was the original, and though one did not find the Speaker's, hm, body, one found this."

I had missed it too, in my original haste to discover what happened to the Speaker. I remembered nearly looking in the desk before Bethaya knocked on the door. *If I'd only had a few more seconds, this all would have been easier to unravel.*

My thoughts went back to the dusty scrap Gompt and I found in the records room. "And older versions...?"

"May now be, hm, conveniently lost."

Then the list would not be revealed to the larger majus community after all, or to the Assembly. We still needed to fix the front gate, but tightness melted from my shoulders.

I tried to hand the paper back, but Moortlin crossed their arms. I frowned. "Why?"

"The Society will be disbanded, and likely sooner than later. One feels the event, hm, happening even now. There is too much damage to the mansion, and the deaths of a speaker and a majus will not go unnoticed."

I still don't understand.

"One will go back to Aben soon, and plant with a suitable group. One has said as much. The Society must be seen as dissolved for many cycles—hm, until all have forgotten about it." Moortlin paused. "Save perhaps the Effature. That one forgets little, though is also, hm, bound by the geas."

I was slowly coming to realize what Moortlin meant. "You want me to keep this secret. For a long time."

Moortlin nodded with a crack of a branch snapping. "Until this one deems the time is right for the Society to, hm, re-emerge. It will be many cycles. This one will be the new head of the Society when that happens. Do not tell the others. One fears a larger group would only, hm, complicate matters."

"Surely there are other, more senior members who are better equipped—"

"Senior, but also, hm, older. This one is one of the youngest, and most capable, members. One can see this one's future will be...interesting."

"I...I don't know what to say." I fumbled with the list, unsure whether to fold it and put it in a pocket, or keep it unbent and frame it, or just lock it in the safest place I could imagine.

"Say nothing. Watch and record the events of the Great Assembly of Species. Decide when the Society of Two Houses should reform to, hm, face the threats of the universe."

Moortlin stepped around me to unchain the door.

Three ten-days after Moortlin gave me the list, I stood, with Gompt and Kratitha, in the rotunda of the Great Assembly. It was my first time on the crystal floor, below the seats of the maji, diplomats, and representatives.

I was surrounded by the sixty-seven chairs of the speakers. Several were empty at any time, and my eyes strayed to the bank of five Etanela speakers, led by the imposing form of Rabata Liinero Humbano. Speaker Thurapo's chair was vacant, as his districts of Etan had not yet picked a replacement.

"You may begin." The voice drew me back to the moment, and I heard the chime of the Ethulina's hoof against the crystal floor. I looked to the Effature, who had said the words. His face was expressionless, the circlet of crystal on his brow reflecting a beam of light shining through the dome.

Don't throw up. Gompt shifted from foot to foot, and even Kratitha was preening her right wing. The left had been amputated last ten-day, but she was already working on a System-based prosthetic to lift her weight off the floor.

"Gathered representatives," I began, trying to keep the prepared words straight. "Today we are here to demonstrate what a System Beast can do."

When Gompt spoke I could barely hear the tremble in her voice. "I am giving the System Beast a few commands," she said, lifting a hatch and flipping several levers. Kratitha wrung her hands as she watched. "In light of the recent tragedy, we thought the creature that helped bring a killer to justice could also give its condolences." Gompt closed the panel and said, "Give your package to Speaker Humbano."

The Ethulina stepped forward, metal hoofs clicking. The glass in its mane caught the light from the dome. There were gasps and conversation as the Ethulina walked across the circle of speakers, stopping in front of Speaker Humbano. Its mouth opened, and from the mobile lips emerged a handwritten note. One hoof split into fingers, took the note, and gave it to the Speaker.

Speaker Humbano frowned, but took the paper, unrolled it, and read it silently. I tried not to mouth the words I had labored over for a full ten-day.

Speaker Humbano rolled the paper up and, surprisingly, addressed the System Beast. "Thank you," she said, "for delivering these heartfelt words. I will see they get to the Speaker's family on Etan."

Her words were the floodgates. Over the next three lightenings—nearly the entire afternoon, we paraded the Ethulina through its paces, and the speakers, the Council, and the Effature debated.

At the end of the demonstration, the Effature addressed us, his warm voice too large for his small frame and balding, elderly head.

"This Assembly agrees to the production and use of what you call System Beasts."

Gompt grabbed my hand in a bone-crushing grip, and my shoulders relaxed for the first time since I had found Speaker Thurapo's body. *We did it. Our concept will be used throughout the ten homeworlds and the Nether.* After all the destruction, there was one bright point.

"But—" Kratitha whispered to us. "Will be a 'but.'"

"But, we would like to see the following adjustments before the speakers all agree to let System Beasts be sold on their homeworlds," the Effature continued.

Kratitha let out a labored sigh. I shook Gompt's paw off before she squashed my fingers.

"The homeworlds of Festuour, Loba, and Methiem wish the displayed intelligence of the System Beast to be reduced. They suggest their homeworlds' citizens will be afraid to use the devices if they perceive them to accommodate their requests too easily."

I heard Kratitha's low-pitched grumble, and tried to ignore the leaden lump growing in my belly.

"In addition, the homeworlds of Mother Hive, Sath Home, and Sureri wish the ability to locate individuals removed or reduced. They fear potential for abuse."

Now Gompt scowled. "So they want a shiny packhorse, is what they mean."

The fine gearing loops of thought, the cognitive functions we'd labored over? Were they all a waste of time? The System Beasts could be so much more than what these speakers wanted, so much *bigger*.

I grasped my thigh with one hand to keep it from balling into a fist, and addressed the Effature. "We can make these changes," I said.

There was still an upside, and I kept it forefront in my mind. Gompt, Kratitha, and I could make System Beasts with all their abilities. The Assembly only restricted us from selling them publicly.

On the way out, Moortlin caught my eye, and waved a wide hand toward themself. I left Gompt and Kratitha with a promise I would meet them at the celebration that evening.

"There was another, hm, decision made today, by the Council of the Maji," Moortlin rumbled when I came close enough. They swung their bald head side to side with a grinding creak as they spoke.

A weight settled in my stomach. "The Society?"

Moortlin nodded with a snapping sound. "It will be disbanded, the mansion condemned. This ten-day."

"What of the—" I broke off as a Lobath speaker strode past. "—of the members and their families? Some haven't been to the Imperium in cycles." *Tethan might not survive moving from the mansion.*

"One has spread the word to the members of the Society. Several families will go into hiding, as those groups chose not to, hm, rejoin the mainstream maji for personal reasons."

Meaning, news of questionable experiments they performed won't be well received.

My hand rose of its own accord to the inside of my fine brown wool jacket, which I had specially cleaned and mended just for the presentation. The list of Society members was tucked inside. *I have the only record of everyone, when they disperse.*

"All this is because of the murders?" I asked.

"Bethaya was, hm, very direct in that one's tale," Moortlin answered. "Though that one listened to one's request to leave certain...others out of the recounting." They raised one finger to my chest.

"And the geas?" I asked.

"There is no *known* way to reverse it, is there?" One of Moortlin's eyes dimmed and brightened in a slow wink. "This will keep unwarranted information from, hm, spreading—a happy side effect."

I watched the Benish's straight-legged stride toward the other members of the Council, wondering at the tightness in my chest. Gompt had already offered me a place to stay with her friend group. We would have to find a new place to work in the Imperium, but the Assembly's agreement to produce the System Beasts also came with a grant of funds.

I silently thanked the Society for helping me. It was disbanded, but not forgotten, and I suspected my knowledge would guide all my future actions in the world of the maji. Someday, the Society would be needed again, be it ten cycles or fifty, and I promised myself I would keep track of its members, both existing and those who could join in the future.

The conviction rose in my chest. The next time the Society of Two Houses emerged, it would be in the open.

If you enjoyed this book, please leave a brief review at your online bookseller of choice. Thanks!

Want more adventures in the Dissolutionverse? You can sign up for my mailing list and get a free short story: "The Symphony Eater."

http://williamctracy.com/mailinglistsignup/

Mandamon Feldo will return in Book Two of the Dissolution Cycle...

ACKNOWLEDGEMENTS

The Dissolutionverse continues growing. I've now published three books and a short story, and the worlds of the Great Assembly are becoming deeper. These novellas let me explore side stories and points in history that might be lost if I tried to include them as a smaller portion of a novel. I'm very pleased Mandamon has gotten his own story. He started out as a character who died off-screen in the first iteration of The Seeds of Dissolution, and somehow graduated up to a member of the Council. Now I get to learn more about his past, writing this novella. This also means you may see a Mandamon point of view in the follow-up to The Seeds of Dissolution.

Kickstarter is proving to be a great way for me to start out with a (relatively) low startup cost for a published book. Making money off of sales, rather than having to pay back my startup costs, helps me focus on writing more stories.

Thus, I am very grateful to the friends, family, and strangers willing to help me fund this project. Because of you, Micah Epstein again created some incredible illustrations, and I was able to work with Luisa Preissler, another amazing artist, who painted the cover. Micah's art can be found online at micahepsteinart.tumblr.com, and Luisa's portfolio is at luisapreissler.de.

Thanks always goes first to my wife Heather, for supporting my writing, and putting up with me when I pay more attention to my writing than to her. She is also an excellent copy-editor! Also, a big thank you to my alpha and beta readers: Eli Freysson, R.K. Bentley, Dan Eavenson, Brook Kuhn, Matt Cote, Vanessa Martinez, and all the folks at Reading Excuses for critiquing my submissions. Thanks especially to J.S. Fields, Robin Duncan, and Laurie Carroll for providing excellent feedback that helped me fine tune the intricacies of this story. Turns out mysteries are hard to write!

Thanks as well go to the members of the Writing Excuses podcast for spending their valuable time teaching and encouraging new writers.

A final thank you goes to my backers on Kickstarter. In no particular order, they are:

David W Hill, Zach Zientek, Mike Goffin, Dan, ThatAnimeSnob, Dhara Henderson Jones, Matt Burris, Sarah Schweitzer, Joseph Rach, Knitdeer, Daniel Eavenson, Rebecca Hogan, Robin Duncan, Martin Ellermeier, Michael Dietrich, Christina Gale, Margaret, Mike A. Weber, Ian Fincham, Brian D Lambert, J.S. Fields, Becky Barnes, Courtney Bowers, Ashley Capes, Ross Newberry, Melissa Shumake, Susie and Ben Roberts, Steve Boykin, William A. Bauer, Clyde Dennis, Christopher Goetting, Zaus, H.N. Klett, Phil Tucker, Jeff Lewis, GMarkC, John Tracy, Scarlett Letter, Brook Whitman Kuhn, Noah Chan, Katie Gomez, Alexandra Matei, Christy Shorey, Austin Alander, Alysse, MXM, Lucas Cooperberg, Romain, Kicklix, Wayne Mathers, David Queen, Anne Burner, Scott and Cindy Kuntzelman, Sierra E-S, Brett M Guth, Hannah, PrintNinja, the Lawrax, Jesse Brown & Michela Munoz, SwordFire, Henry & Julie Burroughs, and Julie Lee.

I hope you enjoy reading!

ABOUT THE AUTHOR

William C. Tracy is a North Carolina native and a lifelong fan of science fiction and fantasy. He has a master's in mechanical engineering, and has both designed and operated heavy construction machinery. He has also trained in Wado-Ryu karate since 2003, and runs his own dojo. He is an avid video and board gamer, a reader, and of course, a writer.

In his spare time, he wrangles three cats. He and his wife enjoy putting their pets in cute little costumes and making them cosplay for the annual Christmas card.

You can visit him at williamctracy.com.

Please take a moment to review this book at your favorite retailer's website, Goodreads, or simply tell your friends!

Made in the USA
Columbia, SC
27 June 2018